★ "Fox writes with force, precision and a fund of sympathy . . . The dialogue is so dead-on it stops you in your tracks and lingers long after."
—S T A R R E D / *School Library Journal*

"Victoria makes a truly wonderful heroine . . . *A Place Apart* is a book apart—quiet-voiced, believable, and often very moving."
—Anne Tyler, *The New York Times Book Review*

"Paula Fox has created another masterpiece."
—*Publishers Weekly*

A National Book Award Winner

A School Library Journal Best Book of the Year

A New York Times Outstanding Book of the Year

A Booklist Children's Reviewers' Choice

A New York Public Library Book for the Teen Age

PAULA FOX

A Place Apart

aerial fiction · Farrar Straus Giroux

Grateful acknowledgment is made to Henry Holt and Co., Inc.
for permission to use the poem "Revelation,"
from *The Poetry of Robert Frost*,
edited by Edward Connery Lathem.

FOR MY SISTER, LOUISE MILES,
AND FOR
ALICE BACH

We make ourselves a place apart
    Behind light words that tease and flout,
But oh, the agitated heart
    Till someone really find us out.

'Tis pity if the case require
    (Or so we say) that in the end
We speak the literal to inspire
    The understanding of a friend.

But so with all, from babes that play
    At hide-and-seek to God afar,
So all who hide too well away
    Must speak and tell us where they are.

ROBERT FROST

A PLACE APART

CHAPTER ONE

A PLACE APART

THREE YEARS AGO, when I was ten, I woke up one morning when it was still dark, thinking that if I could describe one entire day of my life to someone, that person would be able to tell me what on earth life was all about.

When my father died four days after last Thanksgiving, I knew there would never be anyone who could tell me anything. But lately, there's been a change. I've begun to feel that, with help and luck, I could find reasons for the strangeness of events. If someone would only point me in the right direction.

I told my Uncle Philip how perplexed I was and he said that perplexity was one of seven natural conditions of life.

"What are the other six?" I asked him.

"We are too perplexed to discover them," he replied. I wanted to ask him how he knew there were seven conditions of life, but before I could speak, he said, "Victoria, you'll waste a good deal of time if you spend it looking for someone to explain everything to you."

"Will I ever understand anything?" I asked him.

"In flashes," he said. "A glimpse when you least expect it."

He folded up his old green sweater and dropped it in his suitcase. "And in dreams," he added.

"I had a dream last night," I told him. "I dreamed I was a queen, and my crown was a circlet of those little brown pears you can buy in the market in the fall. And I was floating over land that was covered in mist."

"Your dream means that what you must do is find your own country," said Uncle Philip, and he shut his suitcase and set it upright on the floor.

"I wish you could stay a few more days," I said. "Ma doesn't want you to go either."

"I can't leave my business any longer," he said. "Two weeks is a long time for me to be away."

"And there's your cousin Jed, Tory," my mother said as she walked into the small spare room Uncle Philip slept in when he came to help us fix up our house. Ma lit a cigarette and stared at us both through a smoke screen.

"Jed is all right, just bursting to finish school. Lois, why don't you throw those cigarettes out the window?"

"Our yard is not big enough to contain them," Ma answered. Uncle Philip frowned at her. Ma said, "I'll really try to quit this year. Has Jed applied to any colleges yet?"

"He wants to go to Peru for a while," Uncle Philip said. "He wants time off before he gets buried in college."

"Maybe he had a dream that Peru is his country," I said. Uncle Philip smiled and picked up his beret from the foot of the cot, and we all went out to the street, where his panel truck was parked. Ma and he walked with their arms around each other. Even though Uncle Philip is four years older than she, they looked almost like twins at that moment. Perhaps it was because they were feeling the same things—sorry to say goodbye. I was sorry to say goodbye to him, too, but there was something else I felt that I wouldn't have told him about. I was relieved.

Whenever I saw Uncle Philip, or Jed, I couldn't stop thinking of the terrible trouble that had come to both our families. My Aunt Ethel, Uncle Philip's wife, had died three years ago. And now my papa was dead, too.

Ma leaned against the side of the truck and Uncle Philip rested his hand on the door. I wondered if they had ever imagined, when they were children, that they'd grow up and have children of their own, but that the man and woman they had married and had those children with wouldn't be around to see what happened to them.

I wondered where I'd be ten years from this moment, and if I'd remember myself standing here thinking about that faraway future time. I shivered and Uncle Philip suddenly hugged me and said, "I'm off!"

We looked down the street until his truck had vanished from view, then we walked back up the narrow cement

3

path to our house. We stood there a moment. The little houses on Autumn Street looked dingy and ramshackle. There weren't any people out on the sidewalk; there wasn't even a dog.

"It looks like snow," Ma said.

"It always looks like snow here," I said.

Ma clasped my arm. "We'll be all right," she said. "Come on. Let's go inside. I'm freezing." These days, Ma was always saying we'd be all right.

A month after my father died, when we were still in the old house in Boston, she had come to my room in the middle of the night and shaken me awake. I'd sat straight up in bed, my heart thumping. She'd turned on my bedside light and we had stared at each other, neither of us saying a word. I remember how terrible the feeling was that we weren't anywhere we had been before—and morning wasn't going to come, and we were in danger. Suddenly, Ma had said, "We'll be all right." But that time she'd grabbed my hands and asked, "Won't we?" I don't remember what I said, if I said anything. One thing I knew though was when Ma started telling us we'd be all right, it meant she was feeling we wouldn't be.

That's why Uncle Philip had come to stay with us for two weeks. Two months ago, he'd helped us move into our little egg crate of a house in the village of New Oxford. He had come back to help Ma feel better, not just to take up what was left of the torn and muddy-looking linoleum that had once covered the entire floor of the house. I knew

4

it was hard for him to leave his fabric store sixty miles away in Boston. It was a pretty place, full of beautiful material he imported from France and Italy and England. Ma said she had to ask him to leave it, that there were times when she couldn't even make up her mind whether to open or close a window. Then she knew she needed to see her brother.

"It won't always be like this," she had told me just before she telephoned Uncle Philip, "I won't always be like this."

I watched her while she spoke to him and I thought about our house in Boston. I began to imagine that she was really speaking to the people we used to be—only last year but a time that felt a century ago.

That time was sealed away now. When I thought of it, I always saw myself as a very small child. In those days, my mother and father, and Uncle Philip and Aunt Ethel and Jed, had Sunday dinners together. In the summers, we all went down to Cape Cod for picnics on the beach, and on rainy days, Jed and I used to play in the attic of our house. Even though Jed was three years older than I was, he loved that attic as much as I did—the old trunks with lids so heavy it took both of us to lift them, and boxes full of buttons, and heaps of dusty books, and old postcards covered with spidery handwriting, which we tried to decipher, and a stack of hats we pretended had been brought over by the first colonists.

Then, one day when the turkey wishbone was still drying in a cupboard, and there was still one piece of mince pie left over from Thanksgiving, Papa fell down on the sidewalk on his way to work in the high school where he was the principal, and by the time the ambulance came, they told us later, he was dead from a heart attack.

After that it seemed as if our house got emptier day by day, even though people came to keep us company and brought us food. If I was downstairs, I could feel the emptiness on the top floor, and when I was on the top floor, I was afraid the first floor was being boarded up and would look like those condemned buildings I passed on the way to school.

It rained all through Christmas—at least, that's how I remember it—and Ma and I hardly spoke to each other. Every time I looked at her, she had a cigarette in her mouth. She was getting thinner by the day. When she fixed our supper, she'd stand over the stove and stare down at the frying pan until whatever was in it began to send up a smoke signal.

Time passed and all the minutes hurt. I went back to school, where everyone looked sorry for me, and I took a bath now and then and washed my teeth with plain water once in a while, and Ma and I had our silent meals. One night in late January, when I was fighting with my math homework, Ma said we had to sell the house. Papa had not been practical, she told me, and she sounded angry, as though it was Papa's fault for not knowing he would die so suddenly and when he was still young. Not much insurance, she said, and there were a lot of bills mounting up. She sounded strange and hard, as though she were having a fight with someone and knew she was losing.

I started to cry and to shout. We couldn't sell the house! We just couldn't! Ma went and closed herself into her bedroom, and I wandered through the dark rooms all evening. I climbed up to the attic and turned on the weak light and sat down there among the old books and the dust. I knew there was nothing I could do. Our life was changed. It had been two months, then, since Papa had died. I think I hadn't believed it until that moment in the attic. I hadn't believed he'd died for good.

I stayed with Uncle Philip while Ma looked for a new place to live. In the end, she picked New Oxford; first, because she thought it would be a lot cheaper for us to live out of the city and beyond the suburbs of Boston, and second, because Papa had once gone to a boarding school near the village. But later we found out that the school had gone bankrupt and had been turned into a nursing home for old people.

While I was staying with Uncle Philip, Jed came home from his prep school on the weekend. From the way he acted with me, it was hard to believe we'd ever played together and been good friends as well as cousins. That first night, we had an argument about which television program to watch, and it ended with Jed throwing a book—not exactly at me, but in my direction. My uncle sent him to his room. Jed gave me a foul look as he left, and I felt a mean laugh rising up in me. A hint of it must have showed on my face because Uncle Philip looked at me sternly.

"You remind him, Tory," he said.

"Of what?" I asked, but I knew what he was going to say next. And he did.

"Of his mother's death."

"Well—he reminds me, too!" I cried, still feeling mean, but not like laughing. Uncle Philip didn't say anything to me for a long time. I was left alone with my thoughts, which were mostly about how unfair everything was.

The day Ma told me she had found a house on Autumn Street, I felt an odd little thrill. But after we moved into the house on a fierce cold afternoon in February, our old suitcases bulging, the string around the packing boxes frozen stiff, our upright piano sounding terminally out of tune as I hit middle C, and when I saw the rotten planks piled up in the yard near a collapsed shed, and the four miserable stunted apple trees in the front yard, and the yellowed bits of torn lace curtain at the living-room window, the floors covered with gruesome brown linoleum, the iodine-colored cracks in the wall, and the kitchen stove that must have been excavated from the Tigris River after the first flood—my heart sank and the thrill about the name of Autumn Street was all gone.

Somehow, that first evening, we made a meal. We shoveled the grease and rust out of the oven. We walked to a shopping mall on the outskirts of New Oxford and bought pork chops and baking potatoes. And we sat on boxes in the tiny kitchen and ate our supper with our plates on our laps.

"Ma, this is awful!" I said.

"I know it is. But listen! Wait until spring! We can make it better. And the apple trees will bloom. Wait till you see what fresh paint can do!" She put down her fork and lit her hundredth cigarette of the day.

"You won't live to see the trees in bloom," I said, "if you don't quit hammering at yourself with those coffin nails."

Ma started to cry, the tears falling onto her plate, her mouth open, her eyes staring at me. I don't ever remember seeing anyone cry like that except a baby. I felt so alarmed, so frightened! Just the way I had once, long ago, when Papa rented a rowboat to take us for a row on some New Hampshire lake, and when we got out a ways the boat began to sink. That time, Papa had carried me ashore.

Suddenly I grabbed one of Ma's cigarettes from the pack on the floor and I stuck it in my mouth.

"Give me a match!" I shouted.

Ma shut her mouth and snatched the cigarette out of mine. She took hold of my hand.

"Listen, Victoria. The Boston house has been sold, so we've got a bit of money in the bank, enough to help fix this place up and keep us going until I figure out what kind of work I can do. The school you'll be going to is small, and you'll get to know everyone. And it's interesting

9

to live in a village, a real village . . . also, we have a back yard, we didn't have one in Boston—"

"—We didn't have anything in Boston but our beautiful house," I interrupted.

"We are going to *have* to make it all right here," she said.

"Who bought our house?" I asked.

"A realty company," she answered. "They're going to put up an apartment building in our old neighborhood—"

"They're going to knock our house down?" I cried.

She was silent.

I wasn't hungry any more. Finally, I said, "We've burned our ships," remembering something I had read in a history book about Hernando Cortez when he landed on the shores of Mexico.

"Yes," she said quietly. Then she smiled at me, and I smiled back. It was as if a fever had dropped, a fever we had both had for the last two months.

"You'd better unpack a few clothes," she said. "You'll be starting school on Monday." Then she got up and washed the dishes.

That night, we made up our beds where the moving men had left them. We floated like small barges among the debris of everything we owned, boxes of plates and books and pots and pans, albums of photographs, lamps, a few chairs, and the big table that used to be in our dining room in Boston.

"We've got too much stuff," I said to Ma.

"We'll have a yard sale," she replied sleepily.

"Don't smoke in bed," I said. A pale light from a street lamp washed over the room, and I could see a thin trail of smoke rising from somewhere around Ma's pillow.

"Ma? Remember Pompeii!"

"Always . . ." Ma murmured. I saw her heave up and put out her cigarette. I listened to her breathing for a while, and the comfort of it carried me off to sleep.

A new regional school was going to be built just outside New Oxford, I heard later, but the one I found myself in Monday morning looked like an old-fashioned railroad station, one made of dull red bricks and with turrets. Somewhere in the middle of it there was a gym, because at various times during the day I could hear the thunk of a basketball.

No one paid me much attention that first morning except the teachers, who made a special effort to point out to me how much I had missed learning by skipping the fall semester. They weren't unfriendly; they just pronounced their words very loudly when they spoke to me. I ate lunch in the cafeteria, which must have been a classroom in the past; there were still a few desks nailed to the floor.

I played the time game with myself—tomorrow it would be easier; next week I wouldn't remember how strange I felt today; next month it would be as if I'd always been in this school. But sitting there, alone, eating a dry, wizened hot dog and beans as hard as pebbles, I thought to myself, Only the present tense is real, the past and the future are just grammar.

A tall, thin girl with short, dark, curly hair suddenly sat down next to me.

"We're in the same social-studies class," she said. I nodded, my mouth full of beans. "My name is Elizabeth Marx."

"Victoria Finch," I said.

"Are you from around here?"

"Now I am. I used to live in Boston."

"Oh. That little town to the east."

I nodded again.

"In a week, you'll feel better," she said. "And in a month, you'll feel you've always been here."

I said, "That's what I was thinking."

Elizabeth Marx was right. In a month, the strangeness had worn off. I knew most of the other students in the freshman class, and the teachers no longer spoke to me as if I were deaf.

In the shopping mall, Ma and I found a hardware store where we could buy window shades on sale. Everything in those shops and markets was on sale—television sets, shoes, furniture, and clothes. Ma and I put up the shades and felt private, and better. We painted the walls a kind of celery color Uncle Philip had picked out for us, and we had discovered oak floors after the linoleum had been ripped up, so we polished them and put down some small, bright rag rugs. The local piano tuner, who came to tune our upright, was a comedian. When he hit a chord to see what kind of condition the piano was in, he fell down on the floor shouting, "I've been killed!" But he got it into playing shape.

Our living room was just about the size of my old bedroom in Boston, but I could barely recall how horrible it had looked when we had moved in. It was fresh and cheerful now, except it was always a little muddy near the front door, which opened right onto the front yard. We didn't have enough closet space, so Uncle Philip drove over one weekend with an old wardrobe he had found in a Boston junk store. It just fit into my little bedroom; it was like having an extra room. I liked it especially because it had a big iron key that you could lock the door with. There was nothing we could do about the size of the kitchen, but Uncle Philip rescued it from eternal night by putting in a window over the sink so you could look out into the yard when you were washing the dishes. Ma took some money out of the bank and bought a new stove, but we just bought a new rubber stopper for the old lead sink. Ma said she didn't dare trifle with the plumbing in the house. Every time we turned on the water, it sounded as if there were a pond full of croaking bullfrogs in the cellar.

In the early spring, we had a yard sale, and the dining table went, along with a good many other things I had thought I wouldn't be able to bear to part with. We made around $300 from the sale, and afterwards we had an especially good supper on trays in the living room. The house felt light and pleasant. It had stopped being a problem.

Outside, in the light that was lengthening every day, I saw fat sweet buds on the four apple trees. We'd cleaned up the back yard so that Ma could plant a vegetable garden. We knew most of our neighbors now. One of them had told Ma there was a junior college just a few miles from New Oxford that offered extension courses for adults. Ma spent evenings looking through the college catalogue.

"I'd like to earn a living," she said. "I have to. But I'd especially like to be skilled at something."

"You take care of me," I said.

"That's not going to be a lifetime job," she said, smiling.

I didn't want to think about lifetimes.

"I'll take care of you," I said. "Later."

"I don't want to be taken care of," she said, and she looked away from me at a table where my father's picture sat in a silver frame. We didn't have much to say to each other for the rest of the evening.

The next morning, which was Saturday, I woke to hear the wind blowing wildly. I got dressed and drank some grapefruit juice and went to the living-room window. The branches of the apple trees were moving stiffly as the gusts hit them, and there was a kind of pale haze around them even though their buds were not fully opened. Beyond them, I could see Mt. Crystal rising up like a volcano. It was the only real mountain in this part of the country, and the road that led to its peak was about five miles from the village. Forests of evergreens rode up its slopes, and the great rocks near the top glistened in the morning light. It was said to be over three thousand feet high. When I heard that, I gave up the idea of riding my bike to the top. Or to the bottom, for that matter.

I was suddenly aware there were people on the street in front of our house. There was the postman, and Mr. Thames, the old man who lived across the street, and Mrs. O'Connor and her three children, all standing stock-still and staring off in the same direction.

I ran out to see what they were looking at. And there in the sky was a great scarlet kite. It rose and fell like a bird, and I realized I was smiling, like the other people who were standing there, because the whole day seemed to be ringing like a bell, an early spring day, with a scarlet bird for a bell ringer. I could see a small figure standing on the hill at the end of Autumn Street. I walked toward the hill, and the small figure became a boy, his hands guiding the kite as though he were conducting an orchestra. Just as I began to climb the slope, the kite swooped, then fell straight to earth. The boy was winding up the string by the time I reached him. He glanced at me and kept on winding.

"That's a beautiful kite," I shouted into the wind.

He had reached the kite by then, and he was examining it carefully. Then he picked it up and came toward me, the kite held before him like a shield. Buffeted by the wind, it rustled and snapped like something living.

"I made it myself," he said. "When I finished it this morning, I meant to try it out even if a hurricane was blowing." He looked straight up at the sky and smiled.

He was not a small child as I had, at first, thought. He must have been at least sixteen.

"Everyone on the street was watching you—and it," I said.

"Were they?" he asked without interest. He looked at me closely for at least a minute. He had a calm expression on his face; I didn't fidget; I stood as still as a stone.

"You and your mother moved into the Ballard house down the street, didn't you?"

"How did you know?"

"Everybody knows everything in a place this size," he said. "And your last name is a bird of some sort, sparrow? wren?"

"Finch," I said. "My first name is Victoria. Some people call me Tory."

"I'm Hugh Todd," he said, "and I'll call you Victoria."

He was standing next to me now. I saw that he was quite small. But there was a kind of trimness to him that made his height unimportant. And he was not wearing what most of the boys I knew wore. He had on shoes, not sneakers, and a tweed jacket, not a windbreaker.

"Do you live on Autumn Street?" I asked him.

"Oh no," he said quickly, almost as though I'd insulted

him. "My mother's house is up there." He pointed toward the long hill that I walked up every day to get to school. I knew there were several estates there, near the little Matcha River, which flowed through New Oxford.

"I came down here to try out the kite because I've already lost three other kites in our river," he said. For a second, I had the impression that he meant he owned the river. But then I knew that couldn't be true. No one can own a river. And when I thought of it later, it seemed strange to me that he had called his home his "mother's house," yet spoken of the Matcha as "our river."

"I'd like to make a kite," I said. "But it looks so complicated."

"I'll help you if you ever decide to try," he said. We began to walk down the hill, but the wind was blowing my hair all over my face and I stumbled several times. Hugh Todd pushed a piece of kite string into my hand. "Here. Tie your hair up. Quick!"

I gathered up as much of my hair as I could and tied it with the string. By then, we had reached the sidewalk. "You always ought to wear a kite string," he remarked, smiling.

I felt foolish, knowing he was really laughing at me, yet I was pleased, too. He put a finger to his forehead, said, "I'll be seeing you," and walked away, looking straight ahead.

I asked my mother later if she had heard anything about the Todd family. She said she had but nothing much except they were one of the few really rich families in New Oxford, an old family, too, which probably had owned most of the village at a time when oxen still forded the Matcha River.

I told her I had met Hugh and that he'd known about us, known the name of the people who owned the house before we'd moved in.

"Then it's true about gossip in a small place, isn't it?" I asked.

"Yes," she said. "But there's more to it than that. There's hardly anything more interesting than human lives."

That night for the first time since Papa had died, I went to bed feeling really different, feeling there was something to look forward to, not just trudging through the days.

I thought about Hugh Todd, and I was sorry I was so much younger—and so much bigger—than he was. Still, there was something about meeting him on that hill that made me feel the way I had that moment when Ma told me we were moving to Autumn Street.

CHAPTER TWO

SPRING CAME IN DAYS as light as a chain of brightly colored paper rings. New green leaves burst out on the trees around the little houses on Autumn Street and half hid their pinched roofs and tumbledown porches. And Hugh Todd, who now and then walked home with me after school, said it was the best season of the year in New Oxford. "It's the only time you aren't locked in by the hills and the mountain," he said. "It's the time when you know you can get out."

"You make it sound like jail," I said. "Right now it's like a party the whole village is having."

"Some party," he said. "The guests are the old or the middling or the used-up. That's all there are in New Oxford."

We were standing on a little bridge beneath which the

Matcha River curled and mumbled on its course, parallel with Main Street. The water was the color of fishes, green and brown, and gold where the rays of sunlight struck it.

"Who are the used-up?" I asked, staring down at the water, hoping he would start one of his stories.

"They live in houses that look empty," he said. "And they eat turnips for breakfast and listen all day to the peeling of old wallpaper."

"And the middling?"

"They worry that people will think they're used up— so they trim everything, the grass around their houses, shelf paper, their hair, newspaper, wrapping paper, hedges, branches, thickets—"

I began to laugh.

"And the old don't worry about anything any more," he went on. "They sit on stools and face west and don't move all day long."

"Then who can come to the party?" I asked. I watched a little circle of twigs that was being carried on the river's back, and I was half asleep and contented, the way I always felt when Hugh described things to me. It didn't matter whether the things were imaginary or real. They always seemed true.

"Just you and me," he answered.

It was what I had been thinking. Talking the way we were talking, or ambling slowly toward Autumn Street, or looking down at the river was what made the party for me, not only spring. It was becoming friends with Hugh.

One morning, there was a haze of white in our front yard. The apple trees had bloomed, and the air was filled with what looked like a great cloud of pink milkweed.

On my way to school, I passed places I hadn't noticed on the harsh days of winter when the sleet or snow had made me keep my head down and my eyes nearly closed against the cold.

Now I saw tall, narrow houses that looked haunted. I wondered if they were the ones where the middling lived. Once, when I looked up at a small round window, I saw a dog. He was motionless and I thought for an instant it was a painting of a dog. Then I saw him look down at me, actually stare at me! I laughed, but I felt embarrassed.

I passed a block where most of the houses had been abandoned, and the spring breeze stirred the slats of broken fences, and it blew through broken windows and rattled the old paper shades which people had once pulled up in the morning so they could see what the day was going to be like.

It was there that the hill that curved to school began and it took me past the rich section of New Oxford, where Hugh lived. There, the daffodils grew thickly everywhere, and the planting beds had been turned over so the dark earth showed. All along my way, I could hear the waters of the Matcha River, and the air was fragrant and cool as though the river had washed it.

Often, I was lost in thinking about the places I had passed and would be surprised to find myself in front of the school, to see those dark brick walls rising up, and to hear the voices of the boys and girls calling and shouting and laughing until the first bell made everything quiet. There was a mystery about those houses I looked at every morning, and they made me feel a kind of longing I didn't understand.

I tried to tell Ma about it.

"Perhaps it's the mystery of lives," she said. "I have it, too, once in a while. Last week, while I was in Boston to try and get Papa's insurance policy straightened out, I passed a very old deserted factory. I looked up at those big dark windows, all cracked and dusty, and I wanted to go inside and wander around by myself. I wanted to know what it had been like there, who the people were who'd worked there maybe eighty years ago, what they had talked about as they worked alongside each other, those men and women and, probably, children. What had a spring day felt like to them inside that dusty darkness? Is that what you feel?"

"I think so," I answered. I told her about the dog that had looked down at me from the window. Ma laughed and told me she and Papa had had a dog, Ace, when they were first married. "He used to stare at people when we took him for his walks. It was terribly comical. It always rattled them so. We'd found him wandering in the street with a string tied around his neck. And he stared at us in that way he had. So we had to take him in."

"What happened to Ace?"

"He died," she said.

I was silent, thinking of Ace, thinking of Papa.

"He wasn't a young dog, Tory." She stuck a plastic cigarette in her mouth. It was supposed to help her cut down on the real thing. "Ugh!" she said, and lit a real cigarette.

"Are you all right?" she asked me then. "I mean, really?"

I told her I missed Papa, that I would forget he was dead, then suddenly, as though someone had struck me a terrible blow across the back, I would remember. Ordinary things made me miss him, too, when I saw people coming out on their porches after supper to see what the night sky looked like, or when old Mr. Thames across the street went looking for his cat with a flashlight. "Even when I'm laughing at something really funny," I said, "Papa is suddenly in my mind, as though he heard me." I hadn't known, I said, that there were so many ways of missing another person.

She got up and started collecting our supper dishes. I was supposed to do that, but when I stood, she waved me away and said, "Put your feet up and have a cigar."

Later, she went and played some old songs on the piano, songs that had been popular when she was a girl, and she

23

sang along with her playing, making up words when she forgot them. Her light voice was like good lemonade, slightly tart and cool.

Just before I went to bed, I asked her a question that had been in my mind for a long time.

"What about Papa's ashes?"

"They're still at the funeral parlor," she said. "I haven't been able to go and get them. Tory, I don't even know what I'd do with them. They're ashes, not Papa."

I strained to think how he could have become just a handful of something, gray and weightless, without motion.

Ma put her hand on my arm. I looked at her fingers, the strong clean nails, the skin reddish from all the painting and carpentering she'd been doing. "Will you play some more?" I asked her. She nodded. I fell asleep, listening to her playing her songs while my thoughts grew paler and thinner, until they were like the little moon jellies that drifted around in Cape Cod Bay.

I was all right.

Mostly because of Hugh. At first I'd just watched him. Then one day I stopped feeling alone. I wasn't a watcher any more, I'd gotten interested. That interest didn't stop me from missing Papa, but it tugged at me every morning, and got me out of bed fast, and up the hill to school because, that day, I might see Hugh and spend some time with him.

I wasn't doing too badly in school. All French verbs gave me some trouble. And math was a nightmare for me

—especially those problems that went: if your granny was flying a broomstick upstream at 60 miles an hour, and the current was traveling downstream at 22 miles an hour, how many people were in the rowboat?

"You have a profound mistrust of the variable X," the math teacher said, and put me in what the school called an enrichment class, but which I knew—and everyone else who was in it knew—was for math dodoes.

There were a few people I liked, but didn't think much about, and there were a few I didn't like. And there was my close friend, Elizabeth Marx. She was not in my enrichment class; she could square and cube two numbers while I was still adding them up on my fingers. She could play the cello, too. Now and then I stayed after school so I could watch the orchestra rehearse. I didn't really listen. What I liked was to see Elizabeth sitting on the stage, her left foot turned slightly out, her head bent so gravely, the cello between her knees shining like the hindquarters of a chestnut horse.

A sophomore named Frank Wilson, thin and tall and red-headed, seemed to take a big interest in me, and I hated that. All I had to see were his sandy eyelashes and I got mad. Elizabeth said if someone likes you and you don't like them, they can irritate you to death! Once, Frank left a malted milk for me in my locker, and it leaked all over my gym clothes. When I caught up with him, he said, "I broke the world record getting to the drugstore to buy you that in my lunch hour." I was speechless, so I just handed him the leaky carton and turned on my heel, but not before I'd seen a silly smile on his face. Elizabeth said, "Well—he got your attention. That's what he wants."

But it was Hugh Todd who had my attention. I had never thought as much about another human being as I thought about him. It was because of Hugh that I began to enlarge a scene for a play I'd written in my English class. He ran the school theater club, and he had acted in every play the school had put on since he'd been in the fifth grade. The last two years, he'd directed the senior play for graduation. I knew some of the students called him "the Actor." He was good at what he did, and I suppose that was why certain things about him that might have bothered people didn't bother them. After all, he was the Actor, so if he wore whipcords instead of blue jeans, and if he looked bored when people talked about basketball, or if he seemed, at times, to have just a touch of a British accent, like one drop of color in a bowl of water, well—he was different, and good at being different.

Mr. Tate, my English teacher, had us read plays that spring, and when I showed him the ten-page scene I'd written, he said, "It's interesting. I mean that. People often say interesting when they mean boring. I don't. This work of yours really interests me."

I liked Mr. Tate. Now and then he was too cute with us, just to show what a sport he was, but quite a few of the younger teachers were like that. He wasn't a real hony. He wasn't like Mel Mellers, who taught one two-hour class a week to all grades except the eleventh and twelfth. It was called the History of Social Ideas—or, maybe, the Social History of Ideas. Mel Mellers liked to pretend he didn't know any more than we did. One Friday morning he said, "Thomas Jefferson! What a name! Do you dig it!" I didn't dare look at Elizabeth.

Mel, as we were supposed to call him, had a beard you could have hidden three piccolos in. Man! he'd cry, he was really with *us!* Starting out in a world we'd never made! Once in a while, he'd mention his postgraduate work at Princeton. But Mr. Mellers, Mel, was a pal.

Mr. Tate wasn't. I felt he meant what he said. He'd read over what I'd written and mutter to himself, then stab the paper with his finger and say, "That's right . . . Now, here you've gone off . . . you're just filling in space, but not here. Keep at it!"

I told Elizabeth how much I liked writing that scene, how it made up for the torture of mathematics. We were sitting in an empty classroom during the lunch period.

"Can I read it?" she asked.

"It's not half done."

"I'd like to see it anyhow."

"I can't show it to you yet, Elizabeth."

She put half a bar of chocolate on the desk I was sitting at. "Not even for that?" she asked, smiling.

"I can't. Really."

"You make it sound very important."

"No, no . . ." I exclaimed quickly. "It's that I'm scared to have anyone see it. Tate has to. But if I start showing it to you—or other people—"

"—Hugh Todd, you mean."

"—then I won't finish it. You'll like it, or you won't like it, and then I'll start working on it with you in mind. Even if you didn't say a word, I'd be wondering what you thought. Do you see what I mean?"

I couldn't look at her. I was half lying. That means I *was* lying. I had already shown it to Hugh. I wanted to make it right for him. I couldn't have explained that to Elizabeth. I couldn't explain it to myself. It would have hurt her feelings if she had known. We were best friends. But between Hugh and me, there was something else. I couldn't get hold of what it was; what I told myself was that he had a real interest in me. I was someone different for him than I was for Ma, or even had been for Papa when he was alive. When I was with Hugh, I traveled a little distance from myself, and he and I watched and thought about the familiar Victoria Finch who began to seem somewhat unfamiliar.

After I'd first had the idea of writing a scene for English credit, I'd told Hugh about it on one of the afternoons he stopped by my house for a while. Now, when we were both in the lunchroom, he with some of the other juniors in his class, and me with Elizabeth, he'd look straight at me suddenly and I'd look back. We wouldn't smile, or wave, just look. I knew, at those moments, that we

28

ere thinking about the scene I was writing, what he had
egun to call "our play."

I loved to look at Hugh Todd. The whites of his eyes
ere the clearest I'd ever seen, and the irises were like
ark violets. His hair was brown, and it formed dry little
rls over his head. Sometimes I'd go deaf from looking
him, and I'd not hear what he was saying. There was
at smallness of his that I never tired of thinking about,
ose neat perfect hands with clean, shaped fingernails—so
nlike my hands, which were bony, the cuticles gnawed
nd the nails chipped.

When Hugh and I first became friends, I talked to
lizabeth about him, about the way he looked. She never
aid anything one way or another until, one day, after I
ad been going on and on, she suddenly burst out, "Tory!
ll tell you what Hugh Todd looks like to me! He looks
ke the tenor in a rat opera!"

I was speechless. We were cool to each other for a few
ays, but then we got over it. I had had to remind myself
at it often happened that, when you had two friends,
ey couldn't stand each other.

Maybe if Elizabeth hadn't been my friend, she wouldn't
ave felt much of anything about Hugh. But for other
eople, it was as though he were off by himself in some
lace where liking or disliking just didn't count. He didn't
em to come to school so much as he seemed to visit it.

"I guess I know what you mean," Elizabeth was saying.
But I hope you'll let me read your scene some time."

"I probably won't finish it until the fall term," I said. "Mr. Tate wants me to make it longer. And I will show it to you, Elizabeth. Really!"

"I hate to write," she said. "I got Tate to let me do a research paper on the history of New Oxford." She started laughing. "It's got about five sentences of history. I've stretched them out like rubber bands."

I was so relieved she'd given up the idea of seeing the scene that I told her about the first one I'd written and then thrown away.

"I just started to make up a dialogue one day. It was about a man slowly finding out that the murderer he's been tracking is himself. Tate said that was an old, old story, and there was no reason why it couldn't be written again. He just thought it would be a better plan if I wrote about something I knew. So I did."

Elizabeth ate chocolate and said nothing. I don't know why I'm so contrary; I wanted her to ask me what I had written about. I made a face at her calm profile and instantly got into one of those tornado rages at myself which hit me at least once a week. By the time she turned to smile at me, a bit of chocolate sticking to her upper lip, the rage had gone, like hornets veering off in a wind.

"Well, I'm going to tell you," I said, "at least, tell you what it's about. The scene takes place in Boston. It's a rainy day. The daughter is about to go and get the wishbone from the Thanksgiving turkey, which has been drying out in a kitchen cupboard. She has a wish to make. At that

30

oment the shop teacher from the school where the girl's
ther is the principal knocks on the door. He comes into
e living room and tells the family the father has died
the street of a heart attack."

"That's almost what happened to you!" Elizabeth said.

"Tate says that's what's wrong with the scene. He
ys you can't simply write down what happened—unless
u're a reporter. He says you have to burn out your per-
nal feeling in some way. I don't know what he means. But
keep working on it, and it's getting longer, and Tate
ys I'm going in the right direction, whatever that is.
e says I should think of it as a one-act play, not just a
ene. And he asked me what wish the girl wanted to
ake . . . he says when I know what that wish is, the
eling of the scene will be right."

"I don't like wishes," Elizabeth said. I was about to ask
er what she meant by that when Miss Edsey, the science
acher, walked into the room.

"I think you're in the wrong classroom, girls," she said
isply.

"We wanted to talk by ourselves a minute, Miss Edsey,"
lizabeth said.

"I'm sure," said Miss Edsey. "Yes, indeed."

Just before Elizabeth and I parted in the corridor, she
geometry and I to my special math group, Elizabeth
id, "Do you know what she thought we were talking
bout?"

"Love and sex and beauty," I replied.

Elizabeth laughed. "Right!" she said. "They think we'¤
always talking, and thinking, about love and sex—but n¤
beauty."

"It's all those books they read," I said.

Last week, we'd been herded into the auditorium to s¤
a movie about birth. There was a good deal of whisperin¤
and snickering at first. Soon it grew quiet. I could eve¤
hear the rustle of the nurse's uniform when her arm
brushed the doctor's arm. I felt nearly as relieved and gla¤
as the mother looked when they placed that wet littl¤
child on her belly, but at the same time I was thinkin¤
Why don't they let me be?

The "blue hours" is what Elizabeth and I called th¤
hygiene classes, which were taught either by Mr. Chartwe¤
or Miss Battey. I noticed that in no other class did th¤
teachers look at one so straight in the eye. In fact, I ofte¤
got a stiff neck, sitting there, afraid to turn away for fea¤
Miss Battey would think I had private thoughts of my ow¤
about the subject.

After that movie, Mr. Mellers had jumped up on th¤
stage, a brave deed when you considered his weight, an¤
had begun to talk about the beauty of human birth.

In my mind, it was something else, something tha¤
made my heart feel as if it were turning over. Elizabet¤
had whispered to me, "He looks so satisfied with him¤
self—as if he'd laid an egg three times his own size."¤
let out a screech of nervous laughter, and the teacher a¤

32

the end of our row gave me a terrible threatening look as if I'd howled in church.

After all we'd heard in those classes, Elizabeth and I agreed we knew everything and nothing. Names for things. Water is H_2O. H_2O is water. But what *is* water? Elizabeth and I made up stories about round Mr. Mellers pursuing thin, stern Miss Edsey down the empty halls of school at night in the dark, Mr. Mellers shouting, "Beautiful!" and Miss Edsey replying, "Indeed." We'd get sick, laughing. We had other conversations, full of silences, full of questions no one had answered for us, and which we couldn't answer.

The eleventh and twelfth grades didn't have Mr. Mellers' classes in the History of Social Ideas, or the hygiene classes either. But everyone in the school knew him, and we all had to listen to him introduce special programs in assembly. I never said anything about old Mel to Hugh. I knew he'd have seen things about him that would make him look a hundred times more foolish than he already was to Elizabeth and me. Once Hugh went to work on him, I was afraid of the possibility that I wouldn't be able to sit through a Mellers class without exploding into laughter. I knew Hugh was above all that. Or, at least on the other side of it.

I was a few minutes early for class, so I sat down on my books, thinking about all the mistakes I was going to make in the next fifty-five minutes. A pair of green sneakers placed themselves in front of me, and I looked up at Frank Wilson.

"Want to go to the movies Saturday?"

I stood up, feeling at a disadvantage on the floor.

"I can't," I said.

"Too busy with the Actor?" he asked in a mean, jeering voice.

The corridor suddenly filled up with people changing classes, and I turned into the math classroom, not bothering to answer Frank. What he said meant nothing to me, but the way he had said it made me feel fretful and, somehow, at fault. During math, I defended myself against algebra and Frank Wilson, and that day, I lost both battles and ended up talking to myself about the unfairness of everything. Couldn't anyone see that Hugh and I were friends? Yet even when I'd tried to explain to Elizabeth how glad I was to have a friend who was a boy, she'd said, "They're all like Martians."

"They're not so different from us," I'd argued.

"They are absolutely different from us," she'd said with the conviction of teacher stating a principle of algebra.

So there was no one I could tell how proud I was to be Hugh's friend, how I felt *chosen*.

I wasn't seeing as much of Hugh as I had been. He was busy with the graduation play, *Ah, Wilderness!* by Eugene O'Neill. But that afternoon, when I was walking down the long hill toward home, I happened to glance back once and there he was, two blocks behind me. I couldn't tell if he was looking at me or not. I stopped to wait for him. He stopped, too. I was puzzled. I kept on walking, then looked back. He hadn't turned off toward his home, and he was still about two blocks away. He was standing still, his arms straight and stiff at his side. I began to feel very uneasy. "Hugh!" I called.

He didn't move; he didn't call back. All at once he began to walk toward me rapidly. His face had no expression on it at all. When he was standing right in front of me, he opened his mouth and spoke in a flat, cold voice.

"Frank Wilson is a clown," he said.

I felt heat rise in my face like a fever, and I stepped back, away from him.

"I saw you in the hall, sitting at his feet. I saw you talking with him. That kind of stuff doesn't suit you."

"What kind of stuff are you talking about?" I cried, my voice loud and high the way it is when I'm nervous and frightened. Hugh looked around quickly. Only a car was driving by, and just as it passed us, the driver shifted gears with an awful grinding. I thought, Hugh worries about how he looks to other people, even to passing strangers. Then he took hold of my arm and pressed it and started to shake me back and forth. I could feel the strength of his hard little hand, and I was astonished that he had touched me at all.

"His father has been out of work for years, and his

35

mother is a disgusting slob, and he's got three brothers who couldn't make it through the tenth grade," Hugh said in a low voice. "He's not for you."

I shook loose. I could feel tears in my eyes.

"Don't you tell me what to do! Don't you tell me what is or isn't for me!" I cried.

He put one finger against his lips. "Quietly, Victoria," he said. Suddenly he smiled. He let go of my arm and pulled my hair gently.

"That's nice, that braid," he said. "Your mother is good-looking. You're going to be, too. Right this minute, you look like a heron."

"What difference does it make that Frank's father has been out of work? What kind of snob are you anyhow?" I said, but I wasn't shouting now. I didn't even feel angry, only weak. Nothing he'd said really surprised me. I'd always known he was a snob. The worst thing was that it was part of what I liked about him.

"I've got to get back to the rehearsal," he said. "Come on, let's make up." It was as though I'd started the whole thing. "Smile, my birdie," he said.

I guess I smiled, because he saluted me and went back up the hill toward school. It was hard for me to understand what had happened, but there was one thing I knew: Hugh hadn't been jealous, he'd been insulted.

When I got home, I found Ma in the kitchen. Ashes fell from her cigarette onto her sweater. She was slicing a potato so clumsily it was as if she'd never seen one before.

Everyone seemed stupid to me suddenly. I went to my own room and heaved my books at my bed. I felt terrible. I felt murderous. I wondered if the people who decided what special movies to show up in school had a movie about that.

ᘓ CHAPTER THREE

ON A NIGHT a few weeks before the end of school, Hugh telephoned me to ask if he could come by for a while and bring two seniors he'd been working with in the O'Neill play. Ma said it would be all right as long as they didn't stay too late. It was Friday, and I'd done most of my homework. The only thing I had had in mind to do that evening was to try and put together a cardboard model of an Elizabethan theater Uncle Philip had sent me. He'd been giving me models since I was little. I was not good at making them; I wasn't handy with glue or paste, and cutting and matching. I either got the glue in my hair or crusts of paste all over my hands. There would come a moment when I'd start slashing away with the scissors, snipping off those essential little tabs that fit other tabs. What I'd end up with wouldn't be the castle or cathedral or manor house Uncle Philip had given me but a shack for hoboes. But I always felt obliged to try once more.

Grownups get some idea about you in their minds, and it won't go away. "Just keep on working at it, Tory," Uncle Philip would say when he saw the shambles I'd made. "It'll come to you."

Now I stuck the model under a pile of books, took a sneaker of mine from the living-room couch and hurled it into my bedroom, and changed my wrinkled shirt for another shirt that was just as wrinkled but of a different color.

A few minutes later, Hugh arrived with Stanley Bender, who was editor of the school paper, and Carl Meadows, the captain of the basketball team. It was strange to see Hugh with other boys.

Elizabeth had asked me once if I'd noticed that Hugh had no close friends. I'd said, "So what? He's not running in a popularity contest," and she'd replied, "Oh, yes, he is! In a king contest!" Sometimes, I think there are just two questions one is always trying to answer: Is one all right? Or isn't one? For some people, having twenty friends instead of one or two means you're high up on the all-right scale—even if you can't remember all their names. Elizabeth doesn't really think that way, but she didn't understand Hugh. He had less trouble with those two questions than anyone I'd ever known. He didn't need a lot of people clamoring that he was all right.

Stanley was much taller than Hugh, and when he wasn't sitting down, he leaned over himself like a rain-soaked cornstalk. Carl was just as tall, but he stood very straight.

They looked around the living room, nodding and grinning, and the house seemed as small as Hansel and Gretel's cottage.

It was the middle of May but there was a chill in the air. It had rained all day, and through the window I could see the fresh dark-green leaves of the apple trees gleaming with wetness. Inside, the room was warmed by a little Swedish stove Ma had had installed. Ma stayed around for a while, opening the seam of a dress she was altering. The sound of the scissors ripping threads, and the smell of a log burning in the stove, the sense of being safe inside, made the evening feel like winter. After Ma went off to her room with a book, I made a big pot of cocoa and filled a bowl with potato chips. They were gone in two minutes. Then Stanley lit up a French cigarette from a pack he'd bought in Boston. It had a strong, pleasant smell. I picked up the pack and looked at the French words, and I had the feeling we'd all been transported to a foreign city.

Hugh sat in a chair, but Stanley and Carl sprawled on the sofa. At first, I didn't pay much attention to what they were saying—I was too interested in watching them, in hearing the sound of their voices, which rose and fell as they interrupted each other or talked at the same time. They laughed differently. Stanley brayed, and Carl shouted, "Hah! Hah!" and then bowed his head over his chest so the tail end of the laugh was muffled. Hugh would begin by smiling, then he would hold his breath as though the laughter were going backward.

I could see how easy Carl and Stanley were together, but there was something different in their voices when either of them spoke to Hugh. It was a small difference, but it was there. It reminded me of how I felt when I was rattling on to someone I didn't know well, and how, all at once, I'd feel the strangeness of that other person, and then my own strangeness, and my voice would falter and I'd get self-conscious.

Stanley told us about all the poems and stories he had to turn down for the school paper some months, how a kind of plague of awful writing would sweep through the school like an epidemic. He'd have to write poems himself and sign them with names he dug up from thirty-year-old school rolls. If there was one thing he was looking forward to about being through with high school, it was not having to read some composition sent in by a seventh-grader about the planet Grock being invaded by lizardmen with overdeveloped brains.

Carl remarked that he'd written that particular story, and Stanley said everyone wrote that story at least once, and anyhow, Carl hadn't even been in New Oxford when he was in the seventh grade. Then Carl talked about how it was always expected of a tall black boy that he would play basketball, and how he, who was a tall black boy, had been determined to have nothing to do with sports of any kind. But one day, someone stuck a basketball in his hands, and he dribbled it a few feet and heaved it into the basket, and at that instant became captain.

They spoke about music for a while, and Stanley said he'd heard that the three-man rock group that had been hired for the senior graduation party actually lived up on Mt. Crystal in a cave, and all of them slept on stone ledges wrapped up against the cold in their long beards, and that they were able to play the worst rock in the world because of some strange substance they drank which was their only nourishment. Carl said he liked songs from old-fashioned musical comedies. He stood up and suddenly began to sing "I'll See You Again," in a fluttery tenor voice, holding his hand over his heart as though he were making fun of it. I could see that Hugh was crazy about Carl singing that song. He was smiling and holding his breath so long I thought he'd pass out.

For a while they talked about what they wanted to do with their lives. Stanley said he was going to be the editor of the only newspaper in a medium-sized town, and he was going to write editorials to tell his readers what they ought to think. Carl said that for a man who sneered at Grock and the lizardmen, Stanley was taking up the wrong profession. They both looked questioningly at Hugh.

"I'm going to try to survive," he said.

We all stared at the stove for a moment, then Stanley said, "Well, man, that's what we're talking about!"

I went out to the kitchen to get some cookies. When I came back, they were at it again, all interrupting each other, talking about what it would be like to be fifty, about war, about why human beings were so wild to kill each ther, about life on other planets and whether the upper Amazon would be a resort area by the time they were all middle-aged, and about religion, and how long it would take for the polar ice caps to melt, and what was outside of the universe itself.

Stanley ate a handful of cookies and remarked that he'd like to die while he was eating junk food—burgers and fries and fried clams—and that it drove his father crazy because his father was a great cook. Carl started talking about his troubles with mathematics, how it was a language he couldn't learn. And I said that I couldn't do an equation to save my life.

They looked at me in astonishment as though they'd truly forgotten I was there. I was half sorry they'd realized I *was* there. I'd never heard boys talk together the way they'd been talking.

I asked Stanley where he was going to college, and he told me Wisconsin. Carl said he was going to a university in New York and that he wanted to be an archaeologist. Hugh said he wasn't going to go to college for a while. He was going to live in Italy, he thought. We all looked at him.

"What are you going to do there?" asked Stanley.

"Live with an Italian family, perhaps," he replied. "I've been in school thirteen years." I thought, I was eight months old when he started school. He said, "I want time off before they get me."

Stanley said, "Man, we're already *half gotten!*"

Hugh looked at me. "What about you, Victoria?" he asked. "Do you have secret plans?"

"I don't know yet," I said.

"I hear you're writing a really good play," Stanley said.

"It's not a play," I said quickly. I felt a touch of fear and I was surprised by it. Hugh must have talked about the scene to Stanley and that bothered me. So I explained it was just for English credit. Then Hugh suddenly stood up and said he'd forgotten that he had brought along a book he was making and he wanted to show it to us. He was going to illustrate it himself, he said, and have a printer his mother knew make a few copies. It was a book for tired children, a hateful alphabet book, he said, as he took some drawings out of his jacket pocket and spread them on the table near the lamp. We went over to look at them and I passed close by an old pickle crock Ma and I had found in the house when we moved in and which she'd filled that morning with lilacs. I sniffed the scent of the flowers, and the wood smoke and the cocoa, and the joy I felt as I leaned over the table with those boys and looked down at Hugh's work was like the billowing out of a sail when the wind takes it.

A was for Airports, Airedales, Apologies, Actuarial Tables, Accountants. *B* was for Bratwurst, Beaches, Bel Canto, Bovines, Bathos. And there were drawings, odd little squiggles, neat and intricate. Stanley said the Airedale wasn't quite right, but the one for Apologies was very good

And Hugh replied he was better at drawing abstract things than concrete ones. He sounded a bit proud of himself.

After that, they got ready to go. I walked with them to the end of Autumn Street. Hugh whispered to me, "Your house is so nice. It's like something from a Babar story." I was glad that he hadn't said that when Ma was around. She wouldn't have understood; she would have thought he was being patronizing.

When I left them and started back home, they all sang "I'll See You Again," and they sang me past the apple trees and all the way up to the path, and I thought, This is the best night of my life!

The next morning at breakfast, Ma said, "That's an elegant little cricket, that Hugh Todd."

"He's not a bug," I replied.

"I don't know that I really care much for him," she went on while she was cutting the sections of a grapefruit. I realized she was telling me not to care for him either. "I don't like his smile," she said. "It's as though he's watching himself in a mirror all the time."

"Ma, stop! He's a friend of mine!"

"I was telling you what I think."

"You were telling me what I ought to think."

Ma picked up her cup of coffee, drank too fast, choked, and looked at me with her eyes glittering.

"And I didn't ask you," I muttered. I knew I'd better not say another word. But I wanted to fight. I knew it would be a different kind of fighting from what was usual be-

tween us. I felt anger that had an edge like a razor. M
didn't say any more. The sound of our spoons and knive
striking plates was loud, and when I put butter on m
toast, it crackled like a fire. I got more and more uneasy
Bad news was in the air.

But on Monday morning I had good news. I had passe
the math course. Just. It had been like climbing a ladde
carrying two suitcases packed with rocks. That's what
told Hugh that afternoon after school. "You'll always pass
Birdie," he said. "Let's go have a cup of coffee at the Mill.

I told myself I couldn't expect him to take my math
troubles seriously, but I wished he wouldn't call me Birdie
I suspected there was a private joke for him in it—maybe
did look like a bird. But I was happy he'd asked me t
have coffee with him instead of a malted milk, and tha
he sounded so sure of himself, not nervous and boastfu
the way Frank Wilson had when he had asked me to g
to the movies with him.

The Mill was a steamy, narrow lunchroom on Mai
Street with a plastic turkey in the window that had bee
in it ever since I'd come to live in New Oxford. Right nex
to the lunchroom was an old movie house that had see
better days. On Saturdays, it showed cartoons and movie
for little children. Hardly anyone went to it. Instead, peopl
drove to the shopping centers scattered around the country
side where there were theaters built like buses or ai
planes. Often, as I walked by that movie house, I though
of dusty curtains, and cartoons about cats and mice playin

46

the empty seats while a real cat took care of its kittens neath the stage.

"Coffee, please," Hugh ordered in a sharp voice. He dn't even look up at the waitress when she said, "Why— s, sir!" But I did. She was staring at him, and her smile as angry. For a split second, I looked at Hugh sitting ross from me in that booth. He was extracting a paper pkin from its metal container with extreme care, his outh set, a frown wrinkling his brow. What I saw in that cond was how he might appear to someone else, not me, d how old he looked, and I knew he would not change, ally, and the strange thought came to me that he would ver get bigger, only shrink. He smiled, and I saw him as usually saw him.

"Are you really going to go and live in Italy?" I asked.

The waitress put down two cups of coffee in front of e. He drew one toward himself. "The saucer is dirty," he marked.

"Don't tell her," I said hurriedly. The waitress had gone ick to stand near the kitchen door. She was watching us. saw Hugh's small, even teeth gleam in the dim light of e booth. "Please," I said.

"Are you going to let waitresses push you around?" he ked, as if he was making a joke. He began to tip his up of coffee slowly and I thought he was going to pour out on the table.

"Hugh!" I begged, reaching toward his cup. He sudenly righted it. "I hate a mess," he said in a tight voice.

47

He grinned, and began to speak in an ordinary way. "[I] like to live in Italy, or the Outer Hebrides, or Martiniqu[e] I want to do what other people aren't doing," he said.

"But what will you do, if you aren't going to school[?]"

"There are hundreds of programs I can get into. I c[an] go to Florence and learn to cook, or join an archaeologic[al] dig in Anatolia, or study ceramics in Japan. The differenc[e,] one of them, between rich people and poor people is th[at] the rich know how to get a free ride."

It was the first time Hugh had said anything to m[e] about his being rich. Two thoughts collided in my head— how great it was he spoke openly about it and how te[r-] rible it was for him to brag about it. "It's a big differenc[e]" is all that I said.

"Listen, Bird, what I really want to do someday—"

"Don't call me *Bird*," I burst out. "I hate that. I'm tall[er] than anyone in my class and that's bad enough. Ever sin[ce] you started calling me Bird, whenever I look in the mirr[or] I see a stork."

"Put a weight on your head and don't wear feathers[,]" he said; then he grinned and held his breath, and I start[ed] to laugh and forgot to ask him what he really wanted [to] do someday. I was so relieved that he was laughing, to[o,] that I heaped up sugar in my nearly empty cup. I don['t] know why it is with me that relief always leads to swe[et] things to eat.

"You ought to learn to drink coffee black like they [do]

in Italy," Hugh said. "I'll be there this summer. My mother has rented a house on Lake Como. I've been there before, when I was little and my father was alive."

I looked at him in surprise. "I didn't know your father was dead," I said.

"My mother remarried," he said.

"Then you have a stepfather."

"You could call him that."

I had told Hugh, when I first knew him, how my father had died. It often seemed to me that I had told him nearly everything about myself—I was so pleased to hear his voice saying, "Go on . . . go on . . ." in such an encouraging way that I felt I was giving him a present.

I told Elizabeth a lot, too, but with her, telling was a daily custom, and our conversations were like breathing. With Hugh, my life became a story and, it sometimes seemed, about someone I hardly knew.

"When did your father die?" I asked him.

He put down the spoon he'd been holding up to his eye like a monocle.

"He was in California on a business trip. He rented a car and was driving from Los Angeles to San Francisco on the road that goes along the ocean. He went over a cliff and was killed. Near a place called Half Moon Bay."

I gasped. "Finish up your sugar," he said. "I have to go."

I took a quarter from my pocket. He waved the spoon.

"It's on me," he said, and put down some change the way I'd seen people do in movies. I had to make an effort to stop myself from counting it.

We walked together down Main Street. I was thinking how coldly he had spoken about his father and his stepfather. I was thinking how little you could know about another person, and that frightened me. It meant everyone was alone with their secrets.

I could feel him looking at me from time to time. At last he began to speak in a soft, kind voice.

"Listen, I've been thinking about your play. It could be the senior play next year. That gives you plenty of time. What you'll have to do is make it longer and larger. We have to involve as many seniors as we can in it. I can fake some jobs in scenery and lighting and costumes, but the cast must be bigger. Tate will help you. I'll help you. They almost always put on awful old comedies or worse musicals that they buy for a few dollars, things that give everyone a chance to turn around once on a stage before they go off and disappoint their parents for the rest of their lives. Since I've been in school, they've never put on a student's play. It will be a first. If you can finish it next January, that'll give me the spring. It doesn't have to be absolutely standard full length, that would be going too far, but—"

"Stop!" I cried. "I can't do it!"

"Yes, you can, Birdie. I mean, Victoria. You'll do it fine."

"You're like those adults I hate," I said. "The ones who tell you everything is going to be fine, even when you're lying at their feet, blood pouring from a thousand wounds." Yet I felt excited at the thought I could actually write a play, and I could suddenly visualize a program with my name on it, and all the parents and teachers in the auditorium that would become a real theater for one night, and Hugh and me backstage, making sure everything was right.

"You're not wounded," Hugh said. He touched my hair the way he sometimes did, his fingers never touching my face.

"I'll phone," he called back over his shoulder as I turned down Autumn Street. I hoped he wouldn't that night, even though his phone call was always the high point of my day. We would have long, drifting conversations, and even the silences between us seemed full of thoughts. Sometimes Hugh would read me a poem he liked, or make up a story, then hang up just when he got to the dramatic part. Or else he would make fun of some of the people we both knew in school, and I'd have to laugh, even when I knew it was mean laughter. Hugh had a way of seeing what was ridiculous about a person. That's one reason I didn't like him to call me Birdie.

Autumn Street looked skimpy and stale to me that late May afternoon. I wished I was going to Lake Como in Italy, going anywhere that summer. I wanted to take in huge gulps of air and there wasn't enough of it. I felt sad, as though I was being left behind while everyone else went to a party. I longed to be like Hugh, to look out on the world the way he'd looked at me from his booth in the Mill, the way he'd watched Stanley and Carl when they came to my house. I wanted to feel the faraway amusement I knew he felt.

When I opened the door, Ma was playing the piano, dreamy soft playing, full of trills and long chords. She had on her old rough work blue jeans and a sweater that was much too big for her. A cigarette was burning in a little seashell she'd put on the music stand. I suddenly remembered the sweater. It had been Papa's. For a while, I stopped thinking about Hugh.

CHAPTER FOUR

EVERYTHING FALLS APART the last week of school. Exams are over; the books have been read; the problems done. The teachers don't really see you any more—they're looking toward their getaway, toward summer. One morning, a boy from my math class bounded into school, his hands high in the air, a huge pink balloon of bubble gum covering half his face, and he slid down the hall on the waxed floor all the way to the principal's office, where he let out a wild yell as the balloon suddenly flattened. Then he stood there, dreamily pulling the gum off his face, and afterward he drifted into some classroom, looking sleepy. We were all a little like that, wild and vague. It was as if we were stuck on a train between stations—we weren't one place or another. Even Mr. Mellers, our pal, kept his eyes glued on the wall clock instead of on us. Elizabeth and I passed notes to each other about

Mel—about a summer camp, Camp Mellers, we invented, where every morning Mel's disciples gathered to hear him tell how he had invented nature and the galaxies, and all the damp little children lying on their mothers' tired bosoms. Elizabeth wrote that he had a special refrigerator hidden in a cave, and at night he went to the cave and ate mayonnaise sandwiches while his disciples thought he was up on a mountain getting the latest word from the universe.

In the afternoons when I left school, I could hear the orchestra rehearsing. Elizabeth told me the play was not going well; nobody had learned their lines, and Mr. Tate and Hugh Todd raged and shouted at the actors all through rehearsal.

"Does Hugh really shout?"

"In his own way," she answered in that chilly voice she had when Hugh's name came up. "Actually, his voice drops down low and you can hardly hear what he's saying, or else he spits out insults. And you can hear those all right. Yesterday he called Frank Wilson a moron because Frank came into the auditorium to look for a book he thought he'd left there, and he asked him how he was able to find his way to school with such a tiny brain. Frank started to howl at him, and finally Tate just pushed Hugh right off the stage as if he were a little iron statue. But I suppose the play will be okay on graduation day. I hate to say it, but Hugh seems to know what he's doing.

Even if he didn't, he'd get his own way. Rich kids always do."

I had given up fighting with Elizabeth about Hugh. Anyhow, I really didn't know how to defend him. There was truth to what Elizabeth had said about rich kids. They don't expect anyone ever to say no to them. I remember a little girl who had stayed in the same hotel Papa and Ma and I had spent a week in one summer in Nova Scotia. She had been about three years old, pretty and plump, with golden hair. Once or twice, I'd read to her in the afternoons. I was eating a pear one day and she asked me for it—not a bite, the whole rest of the pear. And when I said she could have a bite, her little face got as hard as a pecan shell and she wouldn't speak to me for several days.

I suspected Hugh would look at me like a pecan shell if I ever really said no to him. And although I told myself it was crazy to care about someone you couldn't say *no* to, I liked that hardness in him, just the way I liked his snobbery.

When Elizabeth or my mother, or anyone else, said anything critical about Hugh, I would feel embarrassed and edgy, but terribly interested. Everything seemed true at the same time—all their faultfinding, and all that I felt for him. And no matter how harsh they were about him, I was glad to hear him being talked about at all. I would think about how I loved to look at him, how comic he could be, how joyful I felt when I said something that made him laugh, how important I felt when he was looking at me thoughtfully because he knew I was talking seriously.

I knew when I bored him, or when I was irritating to him. Sometimes, during our evening phone calls, I'd feel restless and run out of things to say, and I had the habit then of saying, "All right, all right . . ." Once I said it five times. And he'd imitate my voice; he'd mock me, and I knew he couldn't stand it. If I bit my knuckles or my nails because I was worried, he'd turn his head away as if I was doing something a little disgusting.

I saw him alone one more time before school ended. We went to the Mill. He seemed nervous and far away. I figured he was worried about how the play was going, so I asked him about it.

"I hate that play," he said. "And Tate was stupid to have suggested it. Nobody is up to O'Neill. They haven't even learned their lines—they flop on the stage like dying fish. They don't care. I don't care."

"Maybe it doesn't matter so much," I said. "It's the graduation that counts."

"Counts for what?" he asked morosely. "Half of them won't go to college, and the other half will stay in school for four or six or even eight years, buried in books, books, books . . . days and years of them. I want to read what I want to read. I don't want to be graded like beef—prime or scraps."

He wasn't looking at me but staring up at the ceiling. I didn't know what to say or do. But suddenly his head came forward and he looked right at me. He made a little hut with his hand, cupping it on the table, his thumb and index finger making a door.

"Here's where we'll go," he said. "This is our little house in Tierra del Fuego."

He made the fingers of his other hand run toward the door of his hand. "That's us. We're coming home from the wild beach, and the breakers are crashing on the sand behind us. And we're going to have a wonderful lunch of Tierra del Fuego lobsters with melted butter made from the milk of the very small Tierra del Fuego cows. And then we'll have coffee that no one but us will ever taste, made from the beans of our coffee bushes, picked by the peons who work for us."

I stared at the cave of his hand for what seemed like many minutes. I didn't know where Tierra del Fuego was. I didn't care. I only wanted to be there.

He lifted his hands from the table and dropped them to his lap. He started smiling, then he snapped his fingers. "Wake up, Victoria," he said. "It was a dream."

"I knew that," I said.

"For a moment, you weren't sure," he said, laughing.

I changed the subject. "When are you coming back from Italy?" I asked.

"Probably the middle of August," he answered. "By then, you'll have finished the play."

"I don't know about that. I'm going to try and get a job this summer."

"You're too young to get any kind of job that matters."

"I don't care about it mattering. I just want to make some money of my own. I'll be fourteen in the fall. There are lots of jobs I can get, clerk in a store, or checkout girl in a supermarket, or run a day camp for little kids—"

"Impresario," he interrupted.

"I don't know what that is," I said. "This is serious to me—getting work this summer."

"You'd better find out what impresario means," he said. "Because that's what I intend to be." I could tell he was making fun of himself, but not quite.

"I'll finish those scenes when I can—"

"They're not scenes. You're writing a play—" he interrupted.

"It's not my whole life," I said. "I don't even like to write."

"I'm renting out our house in Tierra del Fuego. I may even burn it to the ground," he said. "Your play matters. It will matter more than graduation will next year. I'm going to make it the best production that school has ever put on."

I interrupted him then. A question had risen in me that must have been lying in the bottom of my mind a long time. It floated free, perhaps because he had recently talked about being rich, or because, just now, he had spoken of the New Oxford public high school as *that* school, the way you talk about a place you don't like, or where you are an outsider. I asked, "Why don't you go to a private school?"

"There's always been a Todd in that school," he said in a slow, cold way, as if I should have known the answer to my own question. "We keep our hand in," he added. "But I want to talk about your play. The way it opens is right—those children, bored in their house on a rainy day, and their father dying a few blocks away, dying when he's still pretty young, like your father and mine were—and then the telephone ringing. It's the mother who isn't right yet. I've wondered if the mother ought to be there at all. Why not an aunt? Maybe an aunt the children have never met—someone who's been living abroad, in Sicily, or Paris. You want to keep that feeling of strangeness about everything, the way death is strange. All the crying people do just hides the surprise of it, a person disappearing forever..."

"I really miss my father," I said suddenly, and I was afraid I might cry myself.

He got up very fast from his side of the booth and came to sit beside me.

"Listen! I'll miss him, too, if that makes you feel better."

I started to laugh. I felt like a monster, considering what we were talking about. But there it was. I was happy, all at once, and everything seemed wonderful to me.

"All right ... all right ..." I said.

"And stop saying 'all right,' " he commanded.

When we reached the corner where we usually went our separate ways, unless he was coming to visit me, Hugh stepped in front of me.

"Wait. Come to my house. All this time, and you've never seen it."

So that's where we went, up the long hill, and then instead of continuing toward school, we turned left, toward the Matcha River, and walked into the fresh, sweet smell of the water. We passed a long driveway which led to a great stone house with shuttered windows.

"That used to be ours," Hugh said, waving a hand at it. "But my mother sold it after my father died. The Todds once owned this entire hill. Look! See the three small windows on the top floor? Those were my rooms, up there right under the roof. My father read to me every night."

"Papa read to me, too," I said.

"One night, there was a big storm and it drowned out his voice, but while the rain beat down he drew a story for me with my crayons, and after each drawing was done, he'd pass it to me."

"Do you still have them? The drawings?"

"They're lost," he said. "And I've forgotten the story they told."

We had nearly reached the river by then. And I saw a house unlike any other I had ever seen. The most amazing thing about it was the three balconies that hung right over the river. "That's the new house," Hugh said. The remembering, eager sound was gone from his voice now, and he didn't seem much interested in his new house, which he'd brought me to see.

"It's beautiful," I said.

"It's a freak," he said, and then he told me it was a copy of an Italian villa—an architect back in the 1920's had built seven or eight such houses in various New England towns.

On one side, there was a huge garden and white painted iron benches with feet like the feet of animals, and there was a fountain, and near the house, a swimming pool. Where the garden ended, with trellises and climbing vines, a small wood began.

We walked in the front door, and we passed rooms that looked as though no one used them but were filled with a kind of furniture quiet, and a smell of wax everywhere. I thought of Ma's seashell and jar-cap ashtrays as I touched a heavy glass bowl where an amber pipe rested. In niches in the walls were Oriental statues which Hugh said were carved from different kinds of jade. Silky cloth embroidered with flowers covered great wing chairs. The rugs were like beds of flowers, too. And on the walls hung paintings of soldiers, and horses, and rivers bending through tall, slender trees. On a mantel, I saw a clock, and its face was made of tiny squares of blue and white china, and in each square I saw a different scene of people skating, or windmills, or a town square from long ago.

"It comes from Holland," Hugh said. I could have looked at it forever.

We walked through French doors and stood on a stone terrace overlooking the swimming pool. There was no water in it. A few frogs jumped around a drain hole, and a black and orange butterfly wove back and forth across the pool like a shuttle on a loom.

We went inside again, and I went back to the clock. "It's so lovely," I whispered.

"Poor little rich boy!" Hugh's voice suddenly boomed. "Here is the house of the poor little rich boy!" At that moment a door opened and a small woman came in and looked at us. She was wearing a long dress. Its color was a kind of buttery yellow, and the ruffle around the neck cast a pale-yellow glow on her face.

"Hello there, Hugh," she said in a low, pleasant voice.

"This is my friend Victoria, Mother," he said.

She touched my hand with her small, cool one. I was suddenly aware that my shirt was sticking out of my jeans and I wanted, frantically, to stuff it back inside.

"How nice to meet you, Victoria," she said. "Hugh has told me about you. I hear you are writing a fine play."

I mumbled something and stepped back, wishing I could hide behind one of the big chairs. And I felt persecuted. That play again! I wished I'd never begun it. I glanced at Hugh, who was looking out the French doors, and I felt as if he had his hands against my shoulder and was shoving me along a road I didn't want to travel.

"Hugh, why don't you go and get some iced tea and put it on a tray and bring it out to the terrace. We can sit and chat a bit. By the way, your new passport arrived to-day. The picture of you is quite comical. You'll like it." She smiled at Hugh's back, showing teeth that were faintly yellow like her dress. I was glad there was a touch of rust on her.

Hugh turned and looked at her, but he didn't speak. They stood like people acting a charade. I couldn't guess the words. Then someone else came in. He was a tall, thin man, wearing a suit that looked as if it had just come from the cleaner's. He had a thin mustache that grew down around his mouth like parentheses.

"This is my husband, Jeremy Howarth," Hugh's mother said. "Jeremy, this is Victoria. Hugh? What is her last name?"

"Finch," Hugh answered, hardly opening his mouth.

"What a pretty name," remarked Mrs. Howarth, looking at the Dutch clock on the mantel, then at her wristwatch.

"We don't have time for tea, Mother," Hugh said. "Victoria has to go home and practice her oboe."

Jeremy let out a strange giggle. Mrs. Howarth smiled at me and shook her head. "My goodness! A playwright *and* an oboist! What an accomplished child! Isn't she, Jeremy?"

"She doesn't look like a child to me," Jeremy muttered. "She looks like an engineer."

Mrs. Howarth laughed gently, and turned to me, but before she could speak, Hugh grabbed my arm and yanked me out of the room. As we passed Jeremy, I realized he was terribly drunk and that he was clutching the back of a chair to keep himself upright.

I found myself in another large beautiful room. This one was lined with bookcases. A long desk sat in the middle of the floor, and there was nothing on it until I left my fingerprints in the wax.

"Oboe!" I exclaimed.

Hugh put a finger to his lips. "Sssh!" he hissed. Then he pointed silently to the painting of a small child which hung on the wall. I walked over to it while he watched me.

"That's me," he said softly. "I was six."

I put my hand toward the smiling face of little Hugh.

"Don't touch," he said.

"I never knew anyone who had a painting of himself," I said.

"Jeremy plans to have it bleached, scraped, and cut for a vest," he said. I started to smile, but seeing the expression on Hugh's face, I stopped.

We went out into the garden then, and I followed Hugh down the slope to the wood. He gestured toward it. "Jeremy wants to sell off our wood to a developer," he said. "It's the last piece of land we own around here that hasn't had something ugly done to it."

I glanced back at the house. It looked so empty!

"What does an engineer look like?" I asked.

Hugh frowned but didn't answer my question. "Jeremy is drunk by noon every day," he said. "And his brain, if he

64

has one, is rotted out." He told me that his mother had married Howarth eight months after his father's fatal accident, and that he and she had had a terrible fight about it, so terrible he had run away to Boston and gone to a club his father had belonged to, where they let him stay a week. Later, he found out a club official had telephoned his mother as soon as he'd showed up.

"I slept most of the time," he said. "I ordered my meals up to the room so I wouldn't have to see anyone. Then she came and got me. I had to come home. The thing to do is to get through this time—get through it until they can't tell you what to do any more."

I heard a thrush sing. A slight breeze rose and died almost at once, and the late-afternoon sunlight, which lay across the garden and the house, was the color of Mrs. Howarth's dress.

Beneath a maple tree, Hugh stooped and picked up a small branch from the ground. He began to strip off the bark. "He drinks all the liquor in the house, and he fights with her about the hotels where she makes reservations for them. That's about all he does," he said.

"It must be terrible for her," I murmured, but I didn't mean it—Jeremy and Mrs. Howarth seemed like dolls to me, or actors in a movie that isn't interesting enough to make you forget they're only photographs of people.

"Not at all," Hugh said snappishly, hitting the ground with his stick. "She's crazy about him. But I'll be leaving in a year, so I keep the peace. Come on. We'll go through

65

the wood. It takes a little longer to get to your house, but you don't have an oboe to practice, so you don't care. Do you?" He didn't give me a chance to answer but stepped across a thatch of underbrush and in among the trees.

It was a little, musty, dark forest. There was a strong smell of damp and leaf mold in the air. We came to the edge of a pond. It was still and without reflections.

"Beaver pond," Hugh said. "See where they've gnawed the trees?" I saw the marks of animal teeth on the tree trunks, and I touched the raw wood on a small oak. Hugh thrashed about a few feet away. When I looked at him, I saw he was holding a rotted log. He heaved it out into the center of the pond.

"That's rotten Harry," he said. "I think we ought to teach him a lesson, don't you?"

He searched around quickly, found a stone, and flung it at the log.

"Take that, you devil!" he cried. Then he handed me a stick.

I threw it. "You no-good, disgusting Harry!" I shouted.

"Filthy wild pig!" he yelled, hitting the log with another stick. He made a little heap of missiles, and he moved fast, faster than I had ever seen him move, and his face and hands glimmered in the light that was like dusk there among the trees.

"Loathsome dog!" he suddenly screamed and threw a handful of stones at the log.

"Vile viper!" I called.

"Wicked, mean, evil Harry!"

"Fat, dirty hog!"

I was spattered with mud and laughing so hard I was staggering as I turned here and there, bending, and scrabbling at the earth to find objects to hurl.

"Hideous, horrible—" I began, when I realized, all at once, that mine was the only voice in the wood. I dropped the stones and sticks I was holding and looked behind me.

Hugh was leaning against a tree, a thoughtful look on his face. There was hardly any mud on him. I was scared. Something bad had happened, and I had been part of the badness. He saw me staring at him. He smiled.

"I got you going, didn't I?" he said in a light voice.

I felt something for him, at that moment, that was as close to dislike as a worshipper can get.

What were we doing in this little stale wood? Why had I jumped into his game without a thought?

"I'm going," I said roughly. I started off to where I could see the trees thin out. Behind me, I could hear him following, twigs crackling beneath his feet, and my skin prickled and I rushed out into the open. I turned back. He was standing at the edge of the wood, his hands in his pockets, his face as blank as a plate.

He had already begun to turn away when he said, "Good-bye, Victoria."

I ran down the hill to home.

Ma was shellacking an old kitchen chair when I walked into the living room. She asked me if I'd been trying to dig my way to China.

"Rich people are different," I said to her.

She laughed and replied, "There was a well-known conversation about that subject between two famous writers. One said, 'The rich are not like us,' and the other remarked, 'Yes, they have money.' "

"I didn't mean just money," I said.

"You're getting mud all over the floor," she said. "What rich people are you talking about?"

I took off my muddy shoes, but I didn't answer her question. She was kneeling next to the chair, the paintbrush in one hand, a cigarette in the other. She looked kind to me, very kind. I'd never noticed that about the way she looked before.

"What does an engineer look like?" I asked her.

"Like anyone else," she answered. "What a peculiar question! You must have had an interesting afternoon."

I didn't tell her about my afternoon. I didn't tell her about Jeremy Howarth, who, I knew, was nasty whether he was drunk or sober. And I didn't mention Hugh's house, so odd and beautiful, sitting over the river like a fortress, and how mean I thought they all were, Hugh's mother, and her husband, and even Hugh, too, and that the meanness was not only in what they said but in the way they looked and dressed and moved.

I went to the dictionary and looked up the word Hugh had used to describe what he wanted to be someday. *Impresario*. The manager, organizer, or director of an opera or ballet company . . . I had been the impresario's entertainment that afternoon.

I felt thick and restless. A heavy thing had come to burden me; the burden was that I cared so much about Hugh—and I had begun to not want to.

School ended. We all went to see the play. Only the parents went to the evening performance. It was fun to see the people we knew in makeup and clothes that weren't theirs. When the curtain fell, we all applauded for a long time, and everyone who had been involved with putting on the play came out to bow. Except Hugh. Later, I heard that he and his mother and Howarth had left that afternoon for Boston and, I suppose, to go from there to Italy.

During the summer, I got some postcards from him. Most of them were from Florence or Siena or Bellagio on Lake Como, where his mother and Howarth had rented a house. But two of the cards, although they had Italian postmarks, weren't views of Italy.

One was from Disney World in Orlando, Florida, and it said they had a rodent problem in the area and I'd be advised to stay away. The other looked as though he'd found in an attic. It was a cartoon of a baby wearing a big pink bonnet and a frilly pink dress. She was standing on a beach, and in one hand she carried a pail and shovel. The

caption said: *The Beach at Santa Monica*. On the bac
Hugh had written, "Finish that play and I'll make a st
of you!" It was signed: Louis B. Mayer.

Ma told me Louis B. Mayer had been a big movie ma
before I was born, back in the 1930's. I didn't laugh muc
even though I felt Hugh would have expected me t
Ever since the afternoon with rotten Harry in the litt
pond in the wood, I had such contrary feelings about Hug
If I had known how, I would have tried to talk abo
them, to anyone, to a passing horse. I didn't know how.

I didn't do much work on my scenes. Other things can
along to distract me. School seemed far away. I didn't thin
of it. Hugh really was far away. But he was often in m
thoughts, like a toothache in the brain.

CHAPTER FIVE

ELIZABETH AND I didn't have any luck finding jobs. New Oxford was not a center of industry. Once, there must have been little stores, hardware and dry goods and a 5-and-10, and maybe a butcher shop. The big shopping malls had taken most of their customers, and there was no work for us in the few places that hung on, places like the Mill or the bakery or the little grocery store, where there was dust on the tuna-fish cans and the peanut butter was dry and stony. You would have needed an ax to spread it.

We had to start a business of our own, a kind of super baby-sitting. We managed to find eight little children, the youngest being three, whose parents were glad to park them with us for the mornings. Right away, we found out a few things about little kids—they like big pans of water in which they can wash things, their own shoes, for instance, and they like jelly sandwiches to eat as well as to carry in their pockets.

The first week was the hardest because we had no capital to buy equipment with, but the second week, after the parents paid us, we bought a few things, beach balls, shovels with which to dig up Mrs. Marx's begonias, blocks, and a few little trucks. And we made do with odds and ends we found in our houses, rusty pots and wooden spoons and a muffin tin Ma had used to mix paint in. Most of the children tired of things pretty quickly, but there were a couple of loony ones who would keep on doing the same thing until you lifted them up and carried them to something else. Making mud pies, we discovered, was by far the most popular activity. As Ma said, mud cooking wasn't likely to go out of style for a long time.

The afternoons belonged to us. We had our routine. First we went to the village bakery and bought sugar doughnuts. Then we got on our bicycles and rode for miles, stopping to eat our doughnuts when we got tired.

We talked. That was the summer of talking—Elizabeth and I, sitting under a tree, somewhere off a blacktop road, talking about our lives, about ourselves. We got more attached to each other than we'd even been in the spring, and the feeling between us shut out everyone else; just because we were alone inside that feeling, it often made me sad, as though we'd been shipwrecked and only had one another. There were two people I couldn't speak about to Elizabeth. One was Hugh. If I told her the bad thoughts I had about him, I knew she would agree with them. If I told her all the things I loved about him, she would become cold and distant. But I wanted to talk about him! Sometimes I felt I was brimming over like a cup with feelings about Hugh, and there were moments when I almost hated Elizabeth, because she didn't make it possible for me to even say his name. Not unless I was willing to fight with her. When those moments came, I couldn't look at her, I couldn't speak. Then she'd ask, "What's the matter, Tory?" and I'd answer, "Nothing." That's one word that can cover a big territory of *something*. Since there was no one I could talk about Hugh with, I talked to myself about him. Once I tried to draw a picture of him. But I can't draw at all. The clumsy marks of my pencil embarrassed me as much as if he'd been standing there, looking over my shoulder at the drawing.

The other person I didn't mention was Mrs. Marx. She was unlike Elizabeth in every way and I sometimes wondered if Elizabeth had been adopted.

Mrs. Marx was a person made out of electric wires. She seemed to hum with messages you couldn't make out, except you knew they carried news of trouble, of accidents. Often, during our mornings with the little kids, I'd glance up at the Marx house and I'd see Mrs. Marx staring at us from a window, a restless ghost, her eyes glaring and huge like someone who never sleeps. She always asked us questions that sounded as though she suspected us of criminal activities.

For instance, she wouldn't say, What are you going to do this afternoon? Instead, she'd say, "*Now*, what are you two up to?" And once she laughed wildly while she was watching us put away the play-group equipment in the garage.

"Secrets!" she cried. "I know your secrets! I know them all!"

What was strange was that Elizabeth never made any comments about her mother's behavior. But I would see her shoulders droop and her head bow down, and on our bike rides, after such a scene with her mother, she would pedal fiercely and my legs would ache trying to keep up with her. The older I got, the more things there seemed to be that people couldn't talk about, couldn't say. When I thought of myself as a little child, with Papa and Ma, it seemed to me I'd always said everything that came into my head. Maybe I hadn't.

I felt that Elizabeth and I went far away from our homes, our ordinary lives, on our bikes, and that we were like colonists in a country where everything was new. Sometimes, when I got back to my house, after our long rides, it looked so small and dull. I began to hate to clean my room—there didn't seem any point to it, so I'd let things pile up until I had to climb over them to get to my bed, which I shared with books, shoes, and one or two records I couldn't bother to put away.

It seemed a long time ago that Ma and I had talked about old deserted houses and factories and how we felt the same way about their mystery.

There was something new in Ma's life. She'd met

Lawrence Grady at Uncle Philip's on one of her trips to Boston, and, I guess, she must have met him a few times after that, although I didn't ask her.

He looked a good deal older than my father would have been. Elizabeth was at my house once when he came for supper, and she said later that he looked nice. We both knew that *nice* didn't mean much; it was like the X in an equation, just a variable.

Mr. Grady didn't pay much attention to me, and I was relieved at that. Ma tried to get him to. I could see her trying and I didn't want her to. It turned out that he taught in a Boston college, John Milton's poetry, Ma told me. I wondered if we'd ever get out of the school system, and I told Elizabeth I should have been an elementary-school dropout to break the grisly grip of education on the Finch family.

When I looked at Ma looking at Lawrence Grady, she was like someone I hardly knew. He liked her to play the piano for him, and when she played, he'd sit near her and tap his foot on the floor. I wished he wouldn't do that.

Well. He was all right, I guess. Still, when he raced down Autumn Street in his little French car, which you could hear a mile away, and came to spend the evening, I really wanted to be some other place. I tried to explain my feelings to Elizabeth, but they didn't come out right. I remember once that I told Mr. Tate that I knew what I meant but that I didn't know how to say it. Mr. Tate had said, If you don't know how to say it, you *don't* know what you mean. I was glad Ma was so cheerful, but it was a distant gladness.

The dead go away, then they come back stronger than ever. I had been looking in Ma's closet to see if she had any broken-down shoes the little kids could wear for pretending they were grownups. I glanced up at the one shelf, and I saw an old tweed hat. I knew it was Papa's even before I took it down. Ma was out shopping somewhere. I went and sat on her bed and looked at my father's hat. I remembered it.

He had worn it in all kinds of weather, snow and rain and even when the sun was shining on hot days. He'd worn it when we went for a walk one day and he asked me if I'd like to go and have lunch in a restaurant. I don't think I'd eaten in a restaurant before that.

He had taken me to a place out on a pier that stretched its length into Boston Bay. We sat by a window where I could look down at the water, and just before I wiggled into my seat, he waved his hat at it and then at me.

The hat was softened with age, and there were stains around the inside—Papa's sweat, I guess. I got up and put it on my head and went to look in Ma's mirror. I looked like my father. I shivered, and snatched the hat off and buried my face in it a moment, then put it back on the shelf.

Ma asked me, one morning, what I thought of Mr. Grady.

"He's okay," I replied.

"That doesn't sound okay," she said.

"He's not Papa" I cried out.

"No one is," she said.

They often spent Saturdays together in Boston, and I was glad to have the house to myself. On Sundays, he would drive those sixty miles to bring us newspapers and the sweet rolls he bought in some fancy Boston bakery. It was all very comfortable, except for me. I wasn't comfortable.

Elizabeth and I had our hands full with our play group. We had two kids that gave us real trouble. One was Barry, who was four, and had a career in mind based on Attila the Hun's. He would take a shovel in one hand, a pail of dirt in the other, spot an unsuspecting victim, usually a girl, then run to her and dump the dirt in her hair and, at the same time, bang her on the head with the shovel. Someone, somewhere, must have laughed at Barry when he did such a thing. He clearly thought it was a wonderful joke. We told his parents we thought Barry needed a more adventurous atmosphere than we could provide. (We'd learned a thing or two about not quite saying what one means from reading our school reports.)

The other child was our youngest, three, and she bit everything, tree bark, begonias, metal spoons, plates, stones, and passing kitties, but mostly human flesh. She didn't have to be angry to bite, just in the neighborhood

77

of something living. We told her mother that her little
Gladys bit the other children hard enough to leave scars.
Her mother said we'd made it all up—her child wouldn't
do such a thing—who did we think we were anyhow? She
wouldn't dream of exposing her daughter to liars like us.

We ended up with six children, which was really enough,
and we kept the play group going until mid-August. We
got very fond of some of the little kids, but it was marvelous one morning to wake up and know I didn't have
to go and collect our little pack and go to Elizabeth's house,
where we had spent all those mornings protecting the kids
from dire fates.

We each made just over a hundred dollars, subtracting
the expenses for replacing Mrs. Marx's flowers and for our
equipment.

"It feels good, doesn't it? To earn your own money?"
Ma said.

I agreed.

I couldn't think, at the moment, what to do with the
money, so Ma opened a savings account for me, except for
$15 Elizabeth and I had agreed we should each keep for
a day when we would do just as we pleased. Elizabeth
suggested we go to Boston to a movie, or to the Glass
Museum, and look at the store windows, and then have a
real lunch, not hamburgers, but Italian food, which we
both liked especially. Ma said she'd go in with us on the
Boston bus if we'd go on a Saturday. She and Lawrence

Grady wanted to spend some time in Marblehead, and they would meet us in the afternoon and then drive us back to New Oxford.

"What for?" I asked.

"What for what?" Ma asked.

"What's in Marblehead?"

"We just want to look around."

"Look around for what?" I asked.

"Are you cross-examining me, Tory?" she asked.

I burst out, "Well—why are you being so secretive?"

"We all have our secrets," she said. "And our privacy."

I was furious. But I knew Ma's tone. It meant she wouldn't say another thing. I wished Lawrence Grady would move to California. Or disappear from the face of the earth.

When we were walking to the bus station on the following Saturday, I realized Ma and Mr. Grady were going to Marblehead because of something that wasn't there. Me. Just as the bus shelter came into view and I saw Elizabeth standing there waiting for us, I said to Ma, "You want to get away from me."

"You've got it all wrong," Ma said in a firm voice. "But I can't explain it to you, and I'm not going to try."

The heat was terrible that morning. My face stung with perspiration. All of August seemed to have poured itself into the inside of the bus. Ma went to the back, where she could smoke herself to death. I told Elizabeth I thought

79

it was a poor idea to go into the city on such a day, and she snapped back that she didn't want to start off with my complaining. I was mad at everyone and everything for the whole bus ride. Why do days you plan and look forward to turn so sour?

I didn't even say goodbye to Ma when we parted at the Common. Elizabeth and I watched the swan boats for a while, not talking. I wasn't cross now. I was silent, because I had realized that this was the first time I'd been in Boston since we'd moved to New Oxford.

I turned away from Elizabeth then, in a flash, spun around, thinking, Papa is here, I'm small, we've come to see the swan boats! Elizabeth was staring blankly straight ahead of her. I was about to tell her of the mirage I'd just had when three boys on bicycles began to circle around us, whistling and gurgling, and we ran for it while they shouted rotten things at us.

We wandered into a big department store and spent a few moments looking at handbags that cost more than we'd earned with our play group. I was making up my mind which one I wanted when Elizabeth whispered into my ear, "Let's get out of here right now!"

Just as we reached the sidewalk, Elizabeth swayed as though she was going to faint.

"What's the matter?" I cried.

She gripped my arm and said, "I've got to sit down. There's a coffee shop across the street."

We crossed against the lights, and cars honked and drivers yelled at us, but Elizabeth went ahead blindly. Once inside the coffee shop, Elizabeth slumped into a seat. I ordered tea and muffins from the waitress. After a bit, Elizabeth looked at me, then opened her bag and took out a pack of cigarettes.

"The world is going up in smoke," I muttered.

"I wish it would," she said.

I knew now she was going to tell me something I didn't want to hear. I kept on stubbornly talking about how awful cigarettes are for people, until finally Elizabeth said her mother had driven her to them.

"All spring, she kept asking me if I'd started smoking secretly—and she began to kiss me when I came home from school. She's not done that since I was little. One day, I realized she was just sniffing around my face to catch tobacco fumes, and I was hurt and angry. That's when I did start smoking. She goes through my bureau drawers and my pockets, so I hide my packs in the mailbox of an old lady who lives a couple of houses down the street. Once, I got there just as the postman did, and when he opened the mailbox and saw all those cigarettes, he looked so startled—"

I couldn't help laughing. "You should have written an address on them," I said.

But Elizabeth said harshly, "It's not funny. Nothing is funny about what I'm telling you."

"What's the matter with you?" I cried out, my voice much louder than I'd expected. A man in a hard hat at the next table looked over at us. I smiled at him nervously, and nodded as though to say everything was under control.

"I'm going to run away," Elizabeth said. "Today."

"You're kidding!" I exclaimed. I was astonished. I stared at her, at her lovely curly hair I was always wishing I had, at her smooth unbitten fingernails, and then at her sad, sad face.

"I'm not kidding," she said. She smashed out her cigarette and instantly lit up another. I grabbed her hands. She pulled away. I said. "Please, whatever it is, your mother, or something else—just don't smoke those things. You'll get like Ma. She *can't* stop."

She shook her head back and forth in a bewildered way, then she put the cigarette out, and her eyes filled with tears.

"I've got to get away from my mother. That's what it is," she said. "She's at me every minute except when I'm in school or with you. What am I doing? she asks, even when she sees me at the table doing homework. What do you and I talk about? Do I ever see boys after school? In the middle of the night, I see her walking around my room like a phantom. Sometimes she just stands over my bed and stares down at me, and I nearly stop breathing. When Daddy comes home, he hides inside a newspaper, or else he makes a hill of legal documents and then ducks down behind them. At dinner, he tries to talk to me about ordinary things, and she looks at both of us as though she couldn't understand English any more. She'll suddenly shout, 'What do you mean!'"

"You've never told me it was so bad," I said.

"I always told you how she nagged me. And I was ashamed. Besides, you've had Hugh Todd on the brain."

I pushed away my cup of tea.

"Oh, I know you can't help it, thinking about Hugh. I know a person can creep in another person's brain and never leave them alone. Something has crept into my mother's brain. I think she hardly sleeps any more."

"Oh! That's not true!" I cried. "I'm not that way about Hugh. He's my friend just as you're my friend."

Why had my voice gone thin and high? I didn't feel that I was lying. I did have a frantic sense of wanting to hide something. I watched a tear slide down Elizabeth's chin and drop right into her cup of tea. Suddenly I felt glum and hopeless. What can you do if your own thoughts slip away before you can catch them?

"I think about you a lot, too," I said, and then, although I could barely get the words out, I added, "Maybe in not quite the same way as I think about Hugh."

She looked at me humbly and said, "I'm sorry. I didn't mean to do that! It's just what Mom does. Weeks after we've had company, she'll suddenly yell at me for something I did that night that I can't even remember. Now I did it to you. That's what I'm afraid of, that I'll become just like her."

"When did it get so bad?"

"It always has been, but this summer, it's been like a volcano blowing up."

"But she let us have the play group—she didn't complain about the little kids wrecking her garden—"

"Don't you see? She wanted me there, where she could keep an eye on me! Didn't you notice? Whenever I looked up at my house, there she was, standing at the window, staring at me!"

"You can't run away! She'll send the police after you!"

"I don't care!" she wailed suddenly, as she pressed a paper napkin against her face. When she spoke again, it was in a whisper. "I didn't put my money in the bank. I've got it all with me." She wiped her eyes with the napkin. "I'm going to Cape Cod. I can get a job in Provincetown waiting on tables. They've got a thousand restaurants there —and they don't care how old you are as long as you can carry a tray."

"It's too late!" I exclaimed. "It's already the middle of August."

"Oh, Tory!" she burst out. "I'm so embarrassed! About everything!" Then she really did cry. The man in the hard hat leaned over and asked, "Is there something wrong, children?"

"Her pet dog died," I said quickly.

"What a shame!" he said. His sympathy made me feel

84

terribly guilty. "I had a pet once, too, and he died. But you get over it. You get over everything in time."

In time for what? I wondered, as I went to the cashier and paid our check. So many things people said were really strange if you thought about them. I managed to push Elizabeth out to the sidewalk, and we walked here and there, paying no attention to where we were going, and Elizabeth sobbed and people would look at her, then hurriedly turn away. Finally she nearly stopped. She sniffled a few times, then I grabbed her hand. "Look!" I said. We were standing in front of a barber shop, and there was a sign in the window that read: *Haircuts 25 cents, if you're over 95. If you bring your parents, it's free!*

Elizabeth laughed as wildly as she had been crying. So did I. The barber grinned at us through the window. I suddenly wanted to ask Elizabeth if I looked like an engineer. But I didn't. There are a lot of idiotic thoughts you just have to keep to yourself.

She dumped her tear-soaked paper napkins in a trash can and ran her hand through her hair.

"I thought you'd stay with me until the afternoon," she said in a calm voice. "Then I'll take the bus to Provincetown. We used to spend summers there, Mom and me, and Daddy would come down on weekends. I know I can find a room in one of those boardinghouses on Commercial Street."

"What about September? What about school? And your father—"

"I can't think about all that. You shouldn't ask me either. It's like asking someone with a broken leg what they think about the Industrial Revolution."

"What *do* you think about the Industrial Revolution?" I asked. Elizabeth's smile was pale and slight, but it was a smile. She said, "Your mother is nice."

"Nice!" I exclaimed. "What's that? Anyhow, she isn't nice all the time. You'd be surprised. I've been surprised."

We didn't go to the Glass Museum or to a movie because we both realized, at the same moment, that we were fiercely hungry, and when we found an Italian restaurant, we burst through the door as though a pack of wolves was at our heels. But once my hunger pangs had been stopped by a big soup bowl of tortellini, and then by a biscuit tortoni, all I could think about was how to persuade Elizabeth not to run away.

I knew it would end in a calamity. It would be terrible for me—not to have Elizabeth around. And I was helpless with an absolute sense that no matter how old I felt, I was young. My life wasn't in my own hands. I looked at Elizabeth as she scraped the last bit of the tortoni out of its little paper cup with her spoon. She looked so serious. So intent. I thought, You think of running away when you're not free. If you are, you walk away.

After we finished eating, Elizabeth said we'd better go over to the bus station and see about the schedule for Cape Cod. I was getting money out of my change purse. I looked up to ask her if she had a quarter for part of the tip.

My hair nearly stood on end. Elizabeth's face was twice as big as it had been!

It was as though she'd been inflated with a bicycle pump. She saw how I was staring at her, and she put her hands on her face. Then she said one word: "Hives!"

There was no more talk about Cape Cod buses. I got a taxi and took her to the emergency room of the nearest hospital.

The doctor was a young Indian man, and he looked at Elizabeth and said, "Good heavens, child! You look like the moon rising over the Ganges River! What *have* you been eating?"

Elizabeth told him that she had had allergies when she was little but that they hadn't bothered her in years. All she'd eaten was tortellini and tortoni. That was benign food, he said, although it could increase a person's girth. He gave her a shot of something and wrote out a prescription.

We sat for a time in the emergency room so that Dr. Singh could keep an eye on Elizabeth. I watched him listen to the heartbeat of a very old man, and I saw him push back a white lock of the old man's hair from his forehead. The old man put his hand on the doctor's arm and pressed it. Then a mother brought in a little boy with a great jagged cut on his leg, and he cried so terribly while Dr. Singh was stitching him up that I gave up the idea of ever becoming a doctor. The little boy's crying, the old man so pale and exhausted-looking, the smells in that room, made me feel I was just going to topple over and faint, so I was very glad when Dr. Singh came over and looked at Elizabeth and said, "Okay, you can go now. Take care of yourself, Moon."

Elizabeth's face was still slightly swollen when we got to the place where we were to meet Ma and Lawrence Grady. They didn't seem to notice that she looked a bit odd; they didn't even notice we were nearly half an hour late. They looked cheerful and cool and pleased. Mr. Grady suddenly put his arm around my shoulders. I edged away. He instantly removed his arm. I felt apologetic, and I moved back toward him. He didn't try again.

"Did you have a pleasant day?" asked Ma as we got into Mr. Grady's car. "Did you do everything you planned to do?"

"Wonderful!" I said, and I laughed. The sound I made belonged in an attic in a movie about a haunted house. But no one seemed to give it a second thought.

When we dropped Elizabeth off, I looked up at the windows of her house. Now that I knew what I knew, it looked like a huge trap to me, with a spring somewhere in it that would snap shut when Elizabeth stepped over the threshold.

Mr. Grady stayed for supper. I didn't have much to say to him. He asked me to call him Lawrence. I did, once. He was making more of a fuss over me than he ever had. It made me nervous, as if he was trying to overhear what I was thinking about. Ma was stern with me, speaking in short sentences like a telegram. I knew she wished I was more responsive. I couldn't be.

I had a hard time getting to sleep that night. The events of the day repeated themselves over and over in my brain. I felt fretful and a little sick. Finally, I gave up and got out of bed.

There wasn't a breath of air stirring. Each leaf on the trees, and the hard little apples, looked painted and flat and unreal. A moon drifted out of and then behind smoky clouds. Autumn Street was something left over from a war between the worlds, all jagged black shadows and houses that looked caved in. I ate a lot of saltines with jam and drank some stale orange juice. Then I lurched back to bed, caught my toe in a hole in the sheet, then ripped it entirely. I must have slept a little while, because when the telephone rang, I bounded up as if I'd been stung by a wasp. It was just a few minutes before 7 a.m.

I got to the phone before Ma did. She stood in the door to her bedroom, stooped over and looking frightened. I knew what we were both thinking about—the phone call that had brought us the news of Papa's death.

"Yes?" I whispered into the mouthpiece. It was Elizabeth.

"Mom is in the hospital," she said in a level voice. "When I got home, I was too tired to remember to hide those cigarettes. She found them. She started to scream that I was killing myself, so she might as well gobble up all the pills in the medicine chest and kill herself, too. She locked herself in the bathroom. Daddy had to break the door down. I just wanted to tell you . . ." Her voice cracked like a plate and she hung up.

Mrs. Marx stayed in the hospital until the end of the summer. When she came home, Elizabeth told me she was quiet and thin and sad. She never asked Elizabeth anything: not where she'd been, not where she was going or what she was thinking about. She had to take special pills twice a day and she would have to take them for a long time.

Elizabeth said there were two ways, now, that she'd known her mother—crazy and noisy, and sane and silent—and she wondered if there would ever be a third way.

I thought how I had once wanted to describe my entire life to another person and have them explain my secrets to me. It occurred to me now that you had to keep a few secrets to yourself, and that they weighed a good deal. Sometimes, they could drive you crazy.

CHAPTER SIX

EVERY SUMMER, as far back as I can remember, my father and my mother and I had taken a trip. On a morning in August, there would be three suitcases on the front steps, and a picnic basket for our first day's traveling, and a little canvas bag of maps and guides. When I think of those Augusts past, it is like looking at an old patchwork quilt. There are the islands off Cape Cod, and here is the Gaspé Peninsula, or Prince Edward Island, and in the middle of the quilt is an absolutely motionless lake, as blue as a sapphire, and that was in the Adirondack Mountains. Once, we drove south seven hundred miles to Cape Hatteras . . . coastal rats, my father called us.

I remember all those boring hours in the back seat of the car, crumbs in the upholstery from all the crackers I ate, along with the broken bits of crayons I used to color books to pass the time, and on the floor of the car, crumpled and torn pages of comic books that look old five seconds after you've read them. I remember all the stops for gas and food and bathroom, or sometimes just to stretch our legs in some wooded spot where Papa would exclaim over the beer cans and garbage left about, and Ma would calm him down.

The place I remember best was a pond at the end of a narrow gray road in Maine that had led us through a thick forest, and Papa had said that that forest was what the French fur trappers saw, hunters who had come to these parts long before they were settled by other Europeans, traveling across the ocean in long, narrow boats to an unknown land.

We didn't always have a good time. One August, it rained every single day on the island off the coast of Maine that Papa had wanted to visit, and I just wandered around the stony beach tripping over mountains of slimy brown seaweed. At least, that's how I remember it.

Ma and I couldn't manage a long trip. We only had our bicycles. So we decided to take a bus to a village a few miles north of Boston where Ma had heard there was a pretty, old inn built on a cliff over the water. We planned to go for a week.

I liked the idea of going off with my mother and not having to see Lawrence Grady for a few days. There were things about him that made me snarl inside. He had supper with us the night before we left. Ma said she was putting on too much weight, and from now on, she was just going to have coffee and half a grapefruit for breakfast.

"Not me!" said Lawrence Grady. "My breakfast is sacred!"

Imagine anybody thinking their breakfast was sacred! Ma just laughed as though he had made a good joke. I left the table. Wait until I told Hugh about the "sacred breakfast"! I imagined Hugh meeting Lawrence Grady, Hugh, polite and distant, with a slightly amused expression which Mr. Grady wouldn't see at all. And Mr. Grady would be uneasy because Hugh would be so very, very courteous. Afterward, Hugh would imitate him for me, and tell me all the things that were funny about him. Suddenly I felt ashamed. I had a sense of myself bringing people to Hugh so he could chew them up.

In the morning, I looked at our two suitcases by the front door. No picnic basket, no canvas bag of maps, no third suitcase.

"You're not dead," I whispered.

Ma had heard me. "He is," she said, and took my hand in hers.

"It's different for you," I said in sudden anger. "I can't get a new father!"

She picked up her suitcase. "Who can?" she asked. I would have said more but she looked dangerous and I let it drop. We didn't speak much on the trip to Boston.

Just before we changed to the bus traveling north, Ma took a half-empty pack of cigarettes out of her bag.

"Witness this," she said, and dropped the pack into a

93

trash bin. "Now, if you see me sneaking into a tobacco store, you can make a citizen's arrest."

"Do you mean it?"

"I don't know," she replied. "But I'll try."

The vacation seemed to begin right then. Ma talked all the way to Edgewater, the place where we were to spend our week. I saw her glancing frequently at the smokers bathed in their clouds. Then her voice got louder. Talking must have made her feel better. I didn't always listen closely, even though I was interested in her stories about the boarding school she had gone to when she was my age.

I was thinking about Hugh Todd, thinking that here I was, on a lumpy seat in a tattered old bus, and he was probably sitting on a velvet chair in a palace in Italy. I wondered what he was like when he was by himself, walking down a street alone, and if he ever thought of me. I missed him then, with a sharp gloomy missing that didn't seem to have much to do with the thousands of miles between us.

We arrived at Edgewater at twilight. Main Street was only a few blocks long. A spindly handrail ran along the sidewalk on the water side, opposite the little shops that sold magazines or bathing suits. Down below the rocky cliffs, I could see the gray ocean, which lay there like the earth's armor. Our inn was at the north end of the village.

Ma had once told me about five blind philosophers who were touching an elephant, trying to figure out what it was,

94

and each philosopher described the whole animal according to the part he'd got hold of.

I think someone must have hired that same gang to build the inn. It wandered all over the rocks on different levels. None of the windows matched, and we had to spend some time figuring out which, among so many doors, was the entrance.

We went up a long flight of broad creaking stairs to our room. It was big and smelled musty and stale, and the bed coverlets were as thin as paper. But that first evening, when we sat in the dining room, which looked out over the Atlantic, it felt fine, much better than a motel. We were brought little ordinary glasses filled with ordinary tomato juice, but the glasses stood on pretty plates covered with faded flowers and that made it seem like a party. I looked out the big, dusty window next to our table, and I could see lights over the water. It was as though the black sky and the black water were only a thick cloth and those pinpoints of light showed another ocean and another sky that was always light.

The week went slowly for me. I was bored except when I was reading *Wuthering Heights*. Lawrence Grady had given it to me before we left. It was a small book, not much larger than my hand, and I liked its size and neatness nearly as much as I liked the story. With our books, and a bag of apples and cheese, Ma and I would go to the Edgewater beach, a collar of round gray stones at the bottom of the cliffs which we climbed down to on rickety wooden stairs.

It was the first time I remember ever feeling restless alone with my mother. I wrote a long letter to Elizabeth, including two pages I left blank except for a question mark in the middle of each one, and I told her part of my thoughts. I wrote quickly until my fingers began to ache. As I read the letter over, I counted thirty-two *I*'s, so I added a description of some other people in the inn that was so boring it made me groan out loud. In my mind, I wrote to Hugh, and that letter was marvelous and it made him leap from the velvet chair in the palace in Italy and rush to the nearest airport and fly home. I even began the letter in reality, but the moment I had written the two words: Dear Hugh, I flung down the pen and felt my face turn red. My handwriting was childish and, even worse, looked *pudgy!* His writing was neat and clear, each letter formed so distinctly. I was glad I didn't have his address.

On our last evening in Edgewater, after supper, after a long, blue day like the one Hugh had described in Tierra del Fuego, Ma and I took a walk.

The sea was a dark-lilac color, and there was a sickle moon. Other people were out walking, too, along the cliff edge. I suddenly thought of Hugh's father, plunging over a cliff in his rented car, and I felt a stab of fear at the thought of all the things that can happen to a person, and I wondered what might happen to me.

Ma put her arm around my shoulders, and I leaned

against her. I realized that I was as tall as she was, and I would have to stoop to rest my head on her shoulder the way I used to.

"I'm glad we had this week together," she said. "It's been a bit boring, I know, but in a pleasant way, hasn't it?"

I laughed a little, glad she had known how I was feeling and relieved to be distracted from my thoughts. We paused at the stairs that led to the beach. A boy of about twelve, wearing a bright-red sweatshirt, was sitting on the top step, blowing softly into a harmonica.

"Want to go down?" Ma asked.

But I didn't. It looked dark and lonely down there where the little waves breaking made a chalky line against the shore.

"Tory," she said. Her voice had changed. It was solemn. I glanced at her quickly, at her profile, and I saw, just past her forehead, a star that seemed for an instant to be attached to her.

"What would you think if I got married again?" she asked. "Would you find it very hard to take?"

I didn't answer. I wanted time to go backward, just two minutes, to when we'd been silent, listening to the boy play his harmonica. I had known what she was going to say—the way you suddenly hear a tune someone is whistling and you realize that same tune was in your head a second before you heard it.

"Tory," she said again, her voice low and less grave. For a moment, I imagined myself to be a crazy queen who could tell everyone what they had to do: Jump off the cliff! Bring me a golden harp! Never marry again!

At that same moment, an ancient woman, small as a peanut, wearing floppy white tennis shoes that shone in the dusky light, passed us hurriedly. She was singing to herself: *Greensleeves is all my joy* . . .

"The Yankee cuckoo," Ma said.

"I don't know how I feel about your getting married," I said. "I guess it's not up to me." My voice rose as if I was asking a question.

"No. It isn't," she said. "But I care about the way you feel."

I would have to live at home three more years. At home! How would Lawrence Grady fit his big self into our little house? Maybe I would be the one, not Elizabeth, to drop out of school and get a job waiting on tables in Provincetown. Did they have restaurants there in the winter?

"Is he going to move in with us?"

"No. We'll have to find a bigger place. We've been talking about it—"

"—Is that why you went to Marblehead? To look for a place?"

"Yes."

"You didn't tell me."

She looked out at the sea. "I didn't know how to. I don't know how to even now. That's why I just said it."

"His breakfasts are sacred," I muttered.

Ma pretended she hadn't heard that. "We've decided to look in Boston," she said. "You and I can go to school there as well as in New Oxford."

"I'll have to leave Elizabeth," I said, thinking about leaving Hugh. But Hugh himself was going to be leaving in another year. I felt I'd been suddenly dropped back into that empty landscape of my first weeks in New Oxford, and then further back, to those terrible days in our old house in Boston when Ma and I had seemed to drift around like dry leaves. And then I went back years, back to a round kitchen table, and in the middle of it a big glass bowl of floating island, and Papa lifting out the meringues with a spoon and piling my plate with them. I wanted, suddenly, to see Hugh standing in front of me. I wanted to grab his arm and hold on to it so he wouldn't disappear into the future the way Papa had disappeared into the past.

"It won't be until next summer, Tory," Ma said. "Not until you finish the tenth grade."

I knew then the whole thing had been decided. I couldn't lie to myself, tell myself that Ma didn't care about me, but I wished I didn't know that she did. The truth was —there was nothing I could do to change anything.

"Maybe I'll get used to it," I said. But I knew I wouldn't. My mother, my father, me. We were set forever in a picture in my mind. There was a new picture now. I wasn't in it. I could feel my mother looking at me. Once, I looked back at her. I knew she was worried; I could see the frown lines in her face. The boy with the harmonica had disappeared. The star had moved. It seemed hours ago that I had imagined it attached to Ma's forehead.

"Let's go back to the inn," I said. "I want to finish *Wuthering Heights*."

She nodded, and we began to walk slowly back. Neither of us spoke. Now and then I had trouble breathing. It was as if there was a lump of feeling lodged in my throat. The sense of something unfinished between us was hard for me to bear. I wanted to speak, but I didn't know what I wanted to say. Just before we went to bed, I startled myself with an explosion of words.

"Ma. It's not been a year since Papa died," I said. I was looking out the window at the dark sea, my back to her.

"I know that," she said.

"Well . . . it seems so soon for you to get—" but I couldn't say the word "married." It was her fault I felt so embarrassed and angry!

"Look at me," she demanded.

I turned reluctantly. She was sitting on her bed, staring at me.

"I can't answer you. I can't help what you feel," she said. "My life could have turned out differently. I might never have married again. Or not for a few years. I don't know . . . But what happened is that I met Lawrence. I know him and I like him. It's not the way I felt about Papa. It can't be that way again. Maybe it is too soon.

Maybe it's the wrong thing to do. We'll have to see. It's not really you who's taking the chance. Lawrence and I are. Now, come to bed, dear Tory. We have an early bus to catch."

There was nothing more I could say. I stayed awake a long time.

We left Edgewater the next morning and went to Uncle Philip's apartment in Boston, where we were to spend two days, one of which was my birthday.

Uncle Philip had made me a devil's-food cake. It had a ribbon tied to it and a water pistol tied to the ribbon so I could defend it. Elizabeth came, too. I suppose Ma and Uncle Philip had arranged that even before we went to Edgewater. Though I was glad to see her, I felt as if everything was being done behind my back.

My mother gave me a gold chain that had belonged to her mother. Uncle Philip gave me three short novels by Joseph Conrad, Jed gave me a scarf, and Elizabeth gave me a Mexican mirror. The frame was a tin sunburst, and it was just big enough to see your face in.

I looked into it. There I was, Victoria Finch, fourteen years old. For a moment, my father's old tweed hat, the ghost of it, floated just over my head; then it sailed away and I was alone in the mirror. I looked strange to myself, like someone I didn't really know.

Lawrence Grady arrived later, and he brought me a canvas bag I could use for traveling. I wondered what he had in mind. I watched him closely, as though by doing so I could find out what I really felt about him. I knew my mother was watching me watch him.

Perhaps I could have liked him if he and my mother— Suddenly he took my arm and led me off to a corner of Uncle Philip's living room.

"Do you mind a lot?" he asked me.

I thought, They must each carry a telephone in their pockets. How did he know she'd told me?

"I mind a little," I said carefully. We stared at each other.

"I don't blame you for minding," he said. "I'd mind, too, if I were you."

I looked down at the street, at the cars, full of people who were not having this painful conversation.

"I think we can all get along. I want to," he said.

All this understanding! A lot of good it does. Even dentists tell you they're sorry.

"I guess so," was all I could say.

Lawrence Grady drove us back to New Oxford. I half listened from the back seat to their murmurs. I watched Ma lean toward him. I heard them laugh. I felt something I hadn't expected—a kind of cool apartness from them both. It was all settled. My canvas bag was next to me on the seat. I'd use it someday.

A neighbor who had been keeping an eye on the house while we were gone had left our mail on the table. I found a card from Hugh. It was from New York City, a photo-graph of the Empire State Building. Hugh had written only: *The play's the thing*. I didn't care about that. I just cared that he was back, not far away.

School would begin in a week and a half. The mornings were still hot, but the light had a different, thinner weight, and some of the trees along Main Street had lost their leaves.

My scenes were in an envelope on the shelf of my ward-robe. After spending hours on chores I could have done in ten minutes, I finally got enough courage to look at what I'd written. I rushed into my room and flung open the wardrobe door.

There was Ma, sitting on the floor among a lot of old sneakers, puffing away on a cigarette.

I never saw anyone look so embarrassed.

I didn't say a word.

She crawled out on the floor. "It's the first one since I threw away the pack before we went to Edgewater," she said. "I found it in a drawer when I was cleaning out—"

"Why didn't you use your own closet?" I asked, my voice stuffed with the wild laughter that was rising up in me.

"I don't know."

I took down the scenes and went into the living room. Ma was sitting there, still looking mortified.

"Honestly, Tory . . ."

I could see how wonderful it can be to be in the right.

"Is that your play?" she asked weakly.

"I thought I'd better look at it."

"Why don't you read it to me?"

So I did. At first, I couldn't understand much of what I was reading. I was too surprised that I'd managed to put down so many words. After I finished, Ma said, "It's pretty good. How are you going to end it?"

"That's what I've got to figure out before school starts."

"I think the problem with it is that the father's death is the event, and that happens right away."

"When I started writing, I just wanted to describe how that felt. How someone's life can stop—" I could hardly believe we were talking so quietly about what we were really talking about—Papa.

"Then the story has to be about how the living keep on living."

"But—is that a story?"

"It's one of the main stories," Ma said.

That afternoon, Elizabeth rode over on her bike. We stood for a while among the apple trees.

"Mom doesn't even look up when I walk into the room," she told me. "That's not what I wanted either."

I told her about Lawrence and Ma getting married next year.

"I don't like him much," I said. "I don't hate him either. He gave me that traveling bag for my birthday with something in mind."

Elizabeth laughed and said, "I wondered about that."

"We'll have to move to Boston," I said, looking at her.

"I'll come to visit you," Elizabeth said. "We're friends."

We walked down Autumn Street to the big hill. After we'd climbed it, we sat down on the ground, leaning against each other's back.

I could see most of New Oxford from there, and Mt. Crystal, and I even glimpsed the cars, where the sunlight glinted off them, on the main route to Boston. Little children lurched about in the grass, or leaned against their sleepy mothers, whose books and magazines had fallen to the ground, and two dogs chased each other in wide circles. I always thought of the hill as belonging to Hugh. I kicked at some candy wrappers.

"I feel so different," I said at last.

"Yes," Elizabeth said.

"It's almost a year since my father died."

"It's almost two weeks since Mom went crazy."

"Let's go to the bakery and get some doughnuts and take a long ride," I said.

The bakery was out of sugar doughnuts and there was nothing else we wanted. So we got on our bikes and we rode where we felt like riding until the lights began to go on in the houses and you could barely see the tangled fall asters in the gardens. We didn't talk at all. Sometimes Elizabeth rode ahead, and sometimes I did. I left her off at her house and went on home.

Ma said she'd been getting a little worried, it was so late. I told her how Elizabeth and I had ridden about twelve miles without saying a word to each other.

"Since you haven't exercised your vocal cords for so long, how about reading to me while I fix supper?" she suggested.

I read her "Kaa's Hunting" from *The Jungle Books*. It had been my father's favorite chapter and it was mine, too.

I went back to school on the day after Labor Day. Everyone looked changed, even Frank Wilson, who stomped down the hall toward me, grinning. He'd grown a wispy little mustache and he had gotten much bigger. The bottoms of his blue jeans were just above his ankles, and his big bony wrists stuck out of his shirtsleeves.

"How's everything?" he asked.

I'd been looking for Hugh ever since I walked into school, and Frank was in my way. I wanted to get past him, even though I heard and recognized something in his voice that hadn't been in it in the spring—interest in me, not teasing.

"Fine," I said, looking over his shoulder.

"Wait a minute. Talk to me . . . what'd you do all summer?"

"I worked for a while and then I went away for a week with my mother."

"I was in Maine, working in a lumber camp," he said, and he touched his mustache. I had an impulse to ask him if he'd found it in the woods. I thought I glimpsed Hugh among the milling kids at the end of the hall. "See you later," I said to Frank and circled around him. He looked puzzled and uncertain, and I didn't care.

If Hugh had been where I thought I'd seen him, he'd disappeared by the time I got there. Suddenly I was sure he was still in Italy, and I'd never see him or hear from him again. Then I went to my old locker. Inside it, on the bottom, was a bunch of old math papers and a sweater I had thought I'd lost. And hanging from a hook was a package. The paper that covered it was beautiful, a dark leaf-green with flowers like lilies-of-the-valley printed on it. I opened it and found a leather wallet that was the color of a caramel. Little gold letters on the rim spelled out, *Firenze*, and there was a note tucked into it. *Saluti e complimenti*, it read in Hugh's handwriting.

On my way home that afternoon, just as I passed the Congregational Church, I saw him.

He was standing just in front of the glass-fronted board where the times of service and the topics of sermons are printed. We stared at each other across the unmowed yellowing grass. Then he pointed to the bulletin board and smiled. I walked toward him. On the board was the message that Reverend Jeffers was going to preach the following Sunday: *The Many Faces of Love.*

Hugh placed his palms together as though he was praying, then he walked over to me. He'd grown a bit, I guess, not much. I was very conscious of the two inches I'd gained since the spring.

His skin was a lovely olive color.

"Dear Bird," he said, and he kissed my cheek the way grownups have kissed me.

"I love the wallet," I said. "It's beautiful."

He took hold of my hand lightly, and I was startled.

"I thought of you all the time I was in Italy," he said. "There was a little boat I rode that went from Bellagio and traveled up Lake Como, almost all the way into Switzerland, and it stopped at the villages at the feet of the great mountains. I wished you were along. What a wonderful time we could have had!"

"Didn't you have a wonderful time?" I asked. I heard the sharpness in my voice, and I couldn't think why it was there.

"I always went by myself," he went on, not answering me, "and that's the way it was everywhere. Jeremy was learning about Italian wine, and my mother was keeping watch over him. They weren't interested in spending hours on seedy little boats."

He let go of my hand. My palm was damp, but his had been cool. I looked at him. He wasn't really going to tell me anything. Whatever had happened, whatever he had felt about it, would stay buried in him. I would hear only what he chose to tell me.

The time he had talked about the story his father had drawn for him with crayons that night in his old house when the rain fell so heavily, I had understood him. And when we'd flung sticks and stones at rotten Harry in the woods, I had understood something—I'm not sure what—but something.

Yet, I was so glad to see him. Now the fun would begin! That's how he made me feel. That something unexpected and wonderful might happen. Any time. Any day.

CHAPTER SEVEN

ONE EVENING during the first week of school, I was sitting on my bed, staring at the books I'd gotten that day for the new term. The history book was used. I could tell it had gone through a lot of hands. There were mustaches drawn on every person in every picture, even on people who already had mustaches—even on the bowsprit of a nineteenth-century sailing ship. I picked up a thin volume of French short stories. It opened stiffly and smelled of new paper. I happened to glance up then at a poster Ma had had framed for me that hung on the wall over my bed. It was a reproduction of a painting called *The Peaceable Kingdom*. On the glass that covered it was a reflection of my room: the orange glow of my lamp, a shadowy face that was my face. I sat absolutely still, gazing at that other girl. If it was my room, and I was that girl, I thought, I'd be happy. I looked at my real room and at my real hands holding the little French book of tales, which was opened to a drawing of a windmill. *Moulin*, I whispered, and it was as though a spell had been broken.

I felt slightly dizzy and very puzzled. I looked up at the poster again. All I could see was a blurred reflection, and when I tried, in my imagination, to bring back the room and the girl I had seen, it was like grasping a wave in the sea. I heard the phone ring. Ma came to my door.

"Your friend is calling," she said. "Not Elizabeth," she added. She needn't have. I knew from her voice that it was Hugh.

He spoke to me quickly. It was like listening to a telegram. No jokes, no stories. The school newspaper would publish the first scene of my play, he said. I must come to the first meeting of the Drama Club, because the play would be discussed by its members. He had already met with two members, and there would be a good deal to talk about. His voice was as smooth and cold as the touch of marble. Make ten copies of the play, he ordered, nine for the Drama Club and one for the newspaper. The public library had a copying machine, he said.

"You sound like a telegram," I said.

"What!" he said, and the word was like a shot.

"Okay, okay," I said. "I'll do it."

And then he hung up.

I dropped the phone back on its cradle without looking, and it missed and fell to the floor, along with pencils and address book and a scratch pad. Everything lay there in a tangle, the phone buzzing like a June bug when you turn it on its back.

"Tory?" Ma questioned.

I picked up everything and put it back. "There's just too much on the table," I said. "Why do we always pile up everything on little tables?" I went to the window and stared out at the street. I wasn't looking at anything. I was dismayed. It was not the first time Hugh had acted as though he were a million miles away. But when that had happened before, although it had made me nervous and unsure, I had liked it, too. It had made him seem mysterious and private, and I often wanted to be that way myself. This was the first time he had spoken to me like a drill sergeant in a movie.

"Are you okay?" Ma asked.

"Yes. No," I said.

"Shall we take a little walk?"

I nodded. I was ready to do anything that might take me away from my thoughts.

It was a warm evening. Ma and I went down Autumn Street, then to Main Street. Except for the Mill, everything was shut for the night. Light streamed onto the sidewalk from houses, and I could see people walking around their rooms, or sitting down in front of the gray squares of their television sets. Looking at them from the outside, I thought of how you could hardly guess what went on inside other people's lives. I wondered if what I'd seen in my room, in the glass of the painting, was the outside and inside of my own life. By the time Ma and I got back home, I felt better, and we were talking in an ordinary way. She told me she'd decided what she was going to do after we moved to Boston. She had heard of a baccalaureate nursing program that took two years. She liked the idea of being a nurse, she said. She felt it was something she would be able to do.

"After you get married?" I asked.

"At the same time," she said.

Her voice was as sharp as mine had been. I wondered if I'd ever feel calm when Lawrence Grady was the subject between us, directly or indirectly. Why didn't Ma try to make me feel less restless and cranky about him? She sat there, looking as stubborn as I felt. What was she being so stubborn about?

One day, last summer, Elizabeth and I had decided to tell only the truth for six hours. I found out that the truth was not just saying what you felt every minute. It was trying to discover what you did feel that made it so difficult; it was trying to think about what you were really thinking. We had ended up, Elizabeth and I, absolutely silent.

If I said I hated Lawrence, would that be true? No. Well, then? A thick, smoky cloud drifted through my brain. I tried to find a shape in it the way I've tried to see shapes in summer clouds. But the cloud in my mind was not an elephant, or a baby's foot, or a great fish eating up the sunlight. It was a cloud hiding the shape of something else.

"Hold out your hand," Ma said. I did. She put a peeled tangerine on it. I stared at it for a while, then I began to eat it.

"Good?" she asked.

"Good and gone," I answered, swallowing the last piece. And with that, the dark cloud lifted, and I knew what I'd been thinking about behind it. The past, and life with Papa. Good and gone.

There were some surprises in the first month of school. I was put into an ordinary math class that was taught by a new teacher, Mr. Victor. He wasn't ordinary. In our first class, Mr. Victor, as thin as a plank, stood up before us and imitated a digital computer. His eyes were large and round and magnified by thick glasses. By shutting one eye, or the other, or by opening both at the same time, he could perhaps suggest to us, he said, the meaning of the term "binomial." He suddenly jumped from the front of his desk to the side of it. "A quantum leap," he said. He made a pile of paper clips and another of rubber bands, then a combination of the two. "Sets," he said. "The set of clips, the set of rubber bands, and the intersecting set of clips and bands." He asked a boy how many lions were in the room. "None," replied the boy. "That," Mr. Victor cried, "is the empty set. And we are going to study set theory."

After a few weeks with Mr. Victor, I began to see the possibility that there was more to math than the torture of X and Y. The surprise was that for the first time I could remember—all the way back to the first grade and the papers I had handed in with so many erasures they looked like the abominable snowman had been nesting in them—I wasn't scared to walk into class.

The next surprise was to see my own writing, signed with my name, in the first issue of the school paper. I felt proud and embarrassed at the same time—like an intersecting set. The more I read over what I'd written, and I read it a good deal in my room with the door closed, the more embarrassed I felt. But when I was in school and the kids said, "You're in the paper," I felt proud, even though I knew some of them hadn't read what I'd written.

The other surprise was a new sophomore named Tom Kyle.

I was on my way to the Drama Club when I met him. I was feeling important because of a silly thing—being excused from gym. I was alone in the hall, or thought I was, and I circled and skipped down toward the room where the club was meeting. Someone touched one of my outstretched arms. I stopped dead in my tracks. It was a boy I hadn't seen before.

"Listen," he began. I listened, feeling the redness on my face slowly subside. "I've been wandering around the halls for hours! Do you happen to know the room where the Drama Club meets?"

"I'm going there," I said.

"I was getting hysterical," he said as we walked along together. He didn't sound hysterical. It was the first thing I noticed about him, the way his voice went along in a straight line, like a train crossing a prairie. The second thing I noticed was his clothes. Most everyone in school wore jeans and flannel shirts, but theirs were soft and faded and crumpled, and the jeans and shirt Tom Kyle was wearing looked the way they do the minute after you take the pins and price tags off them. I thought of starch. Tom looked permanently starched.

I asked him if he was new this year, and he answered yes. I asked him his name, and he told me that. Nothing more.

In the room where the club met, there were seven or eight people sitting in a circle on straight-backed chairs. Hugh was there, next to an empty chair. He pointed to it. I started forward. But he was not pointing to it for me. It was Tom Kyle who slipped quickly in front of me and went to sit in it. Hugh smiled at me and waved me to another chair.

"Here's the author," he said. At once he turned to Tom and they began to whisper together. I noticed that Tom was small and neat like Hugh, but unlike Hugh, he had long sideburns and they didn't seem to go with the rest of him.

I was sitting next to Lucille Groome, a senior I'd seen in school last year but whom I'd never paid any attention to. She had a long face and reddish hair and she seemed to coil about herself; her legs twisted around each other, and her arms were entwined, and even her fingers were curled.

I wondered if she was older than the other seniors. She acted as though she thought she was.

In the fifty minutes I sat there, Lucille and Hugh and Tom did all the talking. When the time was up and we had to go to our classes, I didn't feel important any more. I threw my gym excuse into the first wastebasket I came across. I tried to get through French class by staring fixedly at my textbook, hoping the teacher wouldn't call on me. I didn't think I'd be able to answer in English, much less in French.

The Drama Club had taken my play apart the way Ma peeled tangerines. How could there be anything left of it? Lucille Groome had said she felt it needed a little romance, and I had protested that it was about a death, and she had said that didn't mean there couldn't be romance, pronouncing that word as if she was jeering at it. Hugh listened to her, and Tom Kyle listened to him as though there was no one else in the room. The awful thing was that the other people sat there like store dummies and didn't say anything at all. The three talkers spoke about new scenes I'd have to write; the play was far too short, they agreed; the mother was out, definitely out, and the aunt who had lived in Sicily was definitely in—

"*What* aunt?" I protested.

"A figure of mystery," Hugh said to Tom.

"Absolutely!" agreed Tom Kyle excitedly.

Lucille Groome looked at me and coiled. "You're a

cute writer," she said. "But the play needs jazzing up. Right?"

"Right!" exclaimed Hugh.

"Right!" echoed Tom.

Even if Hugh had thought all those things that he had said about the play in a voice as cold as a winter wind, it was me he had deserted. He hadn't even defended me against the new boy, Tom Kyle, or that silly girl! Can *anyone* let you down? Would Elizabeth or Jed act as if I weren't real someday? Would Ma? No. Not Ma. I sat there, frozen, staring at the words in the book that could have been written in Persian for all that I understood their meaning. The play! The play! How I hated it this moment! I'd only brought it to the club because Hugh had asked me to. I felt betrayed. It was like being seasick. And the worst of it was that I'd been part of the betrayal.

The bell rang. I got up and left the room without speaking to anyone.

I stopped by Elizabeth's house that afternoon, and while she and I were sitting in the kitchen eating crackers and cheese, Mrs. Marx came in and asked us if we'd found anything to eat, then drifted out.

"Those pills she takes make her dopey," she said. She looked so somber, so unhappy, my own trouble seemed less important. I couldn't put it aside for long, though, so I told her what had happened.

"All you have to do, Tory, is to say they can't have what you've written. Then take that play and bury it somewhere.

It's been trouble for you since Hugh got hold of it. Take it away from him It's simple!"

That's just what it wasn't. Simple. The idea of telling Hugh that I couldn't write any more, that I was through with the whole thing, made me feel ill. If only I'd never begun it!

"It's Hugh and what he'll think that worries you, isn't it?"

I nodded.

"Hugh!" Elizabeth suddenly exploded. Her face crinkled up and she looked fierce.

"He said he liked it so much, he said—"

"Said!" she interrupted. "Hugh would say anything. But Hugh wouldn't have to mean what he says."

"But he did mean it!" I insisted. "You don't understand. You're tangling everything up because you don't like him."

"I've known him since the first grade," she said. "He's always been a fake—he just gets better at it. People like Hugh only want to look different from everyone else—on the outside. Inside, Hugh's a hundred times greedier and meaner than anyone I know! I still remember what he did when we were both in third grade and I brought in some cupcakes for a class birthday party. When no one was looking, he ate four of them. But the awful thing was, he took bites out of all the rest of them! Then he said I'd given them to him!"

I started to laugh, but I could hear my laughter and it was choked and angry.

"Lucille Groome told me I was a cute writer," I said, and I kept on laughing like a fool.

"In the seventh grade Lucille Groome had a crush on Mel Mellers!" Elizabeth said.

I fell onto the table, blowing cracker crumbs all over the floor.

"Can you imagine?" asked Elizabeth.

"Yes," I said weakly.

"You go see Mr. Tate tomorrow and call the whole thing off," she said.

"I can't yet," I said, thinking the Drama Club would call the whole thing off for me if things went on as they had started that day.

"Hugh is smart," I said suddenly, surprising myself.

"Being smart isn't everything," Elizabeth said sadly. "My mother was smart."

On my way home, I thought how what Elizabeth had said, the advice she had given me, didn't match up with the trouble I had. Maybe advice was often like that—a key to a door, but not the door you were locked behind.

Old Mr. Thames called out to me just before I went up the path to the house.

"I've lost Benny again," he told me.

"Benny always comes home," I said, noticing that Mr. Thames was carrying a flashlight although it was still broad daylight.

"He's been gone all day," he said, and he sighed. "That

cat drives me mad," he said. Benny drove quite a few people mad. He was always walking into people's houses and curling up in a bed like Goldilocks. I had found him, several times, in my bed, his head on my pillow like a person's, a big orange and white cat head, his whiskers whiffling as he slept.

At that moment, Benny crawled out from Mr. Thames's hedge.

"You devil!" cried Mr. Thames.

Benny made a figure eight out of himself, then raced into the house through the open door. Mr. Thames grinned. "A darling cat," he said, "but unreliable. Thanks, Victoria. I'd hate to lose him."

Unreliable, I thought to myself. Everything was unreliable.

A little after nine o'clock that evening, Hugh telephoned.

"Have you recovered from the critics?" he asked. I listened intently to his voice. It was confidential. It seemed to say that there were just two of us who mattered, two of us being private. For the first time, I felt outside of our conversation. I felt wary.

"Do you really agree with that girl?" I asked loudly. "What *was* she talking about?"

"Lucille?" he asked. "Lucille is a good actress. She's always been in the school plays. I don't completely agree with her. But there was something to it. You and I know there isn't much plot to the play. That's all she meant."

I drew two bicycle wheels on the pad next to the phone.

"Victoria? If you're going to write, you have to get used to criticism," he said.

"I can't make the play longer. I don't want to," I said.

I couldn't hear him breathing. Perhaps he was drawing on a pad, too. A hangman's noose for me.

"Hugh? I'm sorry. I can't do it."

"You have to," he said. "I've counted on it. I know just how it will be."

I said nothing. I stared at Ma, who was sitting at the table reading something. She turned suddenly and looked at me, and then raised her eyebrows as though questioning me. I don't know how I looked, but she stood up and started to walk to me. I waved her back. Stammering, I asked the telephone who Tom Kyle was. I was really startled when Hugh spoke; I'd been convinced there was no one there. He replied as though there had been no argument between us. He told me the Kyles were from Boston, that they'd bought the old Cass farm and were fixing it up, and that Tom's father had an advertising agency in the city. Tom had gone to a private school. His mother had been a professional actress.

"What is she now?" I asked.

"A cripple," he said. "She has rheumatoid arthritis. That's why they've moved out of Boston, to the country."

I didn't see what Hugh's *why* connected; I just wished the Kyles had stayed in Boston. I couldn't ask the question that was like a thorn in my mind. Why had Hugh pointed at the chair next to him at the Drama Club meeting and waved Tom to it?

"Birdie?" He spoke softly now. "There's a terrific Marx Brothers' movie on the tube tonight. Do you want to watch it?"

"I've seen all their movies," I said. "Years ago. My father loved them and took me when they showed a bunch of them in Boston."

"I love them, too," he said. "And I love your play. We'll talk about it tomorrow. All right? See, I can say 'all right' just the way you do. Now I'm going to hang up because the movie is about to start."

He hadn't believed what I'd said. He didn't believe I wouldn't write more for him. Or else he refused to believe it. But I felt a little better, just because I'd told him I wasn't going to.

"What's up?" Ma asked me.

"Nothing," I said.

I looked out the living-room window. I saw the beam of Mr. Thames's flashlight poking beneath the hedge. Benny had gotten out again.

"Will you watch an old movie with me?" I asked Ma.

"Sure," she said.

We went to her room, where our old television set sat on its stand in the corner, and we fixed up pillows and got on her bed. She kept her arm around my shoulders while we watched, and we laughed a good deal. By the time I went to bed, I felt almost calm, even though Tom Kyle's name kept floating through my mind, a worry I couldn't put a name to.

Hugh was waiting for me by the Congregational Church after school the next day. There was a certain expression on his face that I'd often seen before, and that I loved. It was a sweet look and it was humorous, too, as though he was thinking about something funny that he couldn't wait to tell me about. I suppose I'd thought, after the meeting in the Drama Club, when he'd deserted me, when I'd felt so mortified by myself, that it would be easy to be cool with him, that all at once I wouldn't trust him any more. But that's not the way it was—perhaps it never could be that way. Along with the new feeling I had about him, the caution I felt toward him, the old feelings were still there. He could still get me. If people were like numbers, they'd just be one thing—a seven or a twelve. But the only numbers they seemed to be like were variables. I knew I was smiling at him now, smiling at him in the old way because I was feeling about him in the old way.

"Listen!" he began, "remember the scene when Groucho thinks he's looking at his reflection in a mirror only it's Harpo dressed up to look like him?"

I laughed, remembering, and nodded.

"Let's do it!" he said. "Come on!"

He stood in front of me and slowly raised his eyebrows, and I raised mine.

He slowly stretched out his right arm. I did the same.

"Faster!" he whispered.

I saw his leg rise and I lifted mine, and he hopped and I did, and then he pretended he was wiping fog from the mirror and I did it right on time. He turned in a circle and I did, and he did it again, then walked away from me. I walked away from him, laughing. I finally turned back. He was gone.

I ran behind the church and into the cemetery. He wasn't there. He wasn't behind a tombstone. He was nowhere.

A squirrel darted across the grass and up a tree. Some of the tombstones were ancient and had fallen sideways. Green moss covered them like the stitches on an old needlepoint pillow Ma had on a chair in her bedroom. I stopped and began to read the engraving on a tombstone. A leaf drifted down from a maple tree and landed in my hair. I couldn't hear cars or voices, only a faint, sighing breeze way up in the top branches of the trees.

Letitia Cass, 1834–1865, I read. There was something written in Latin, too, but it was half buried. She must have been a member of the family which had owned the house Tom Kyle had moved into.

I sat under a tree for a while, thinking about the people buried all around me who had once been breathing in the October air, expecting this and hoping for that, and worrying sometimes, the way I was worrying.

I felt quiet and sad and confused. Hugh hadn't mentioned the play. It was as though he had decided everything was settled. I would have to go against him; I would have to settle my own part of it.

Hugh's jokes weren't like other people's. You were really allowed to see only half of a joke. The rest of it was buried in him, like the Latin words on the Cass tombstone. His disappearing the way he had was just like the way he would suddenly hang up the phone when he was in the middle of a story. It wasn't funny to me now. I felt I wouldn't find him ever again.

I picked up my books and walked out of the cemetery. I would have liked to stay there a long time with the squirrel and the trees and the old graves.

On Main Street, a few people were heading toward the library, carrying their books and wearing the library expression, pensive and dreamy. Others shopped in the bakery and the grocery store, and the usual gang was hanging around beneath the marquee of the movie house. As I passed by the Mill, I glanced in as I always did, just because Hugh and I had had good times there.

When I saw Tom Kyle and Hugh sitting in the booth, talking, I quickened my step. I told myself I didn't want Hugh to see me, but a second later I realized I didn't want Hugh to know I'd seen him. Why would that matter? Why did I feel so embarrassed? Oh, if only I could stop thinking!

Frank Wilson suddenly stepped out from the group of boys near the boarded-up old box office of the movie.

"Vicky, how about a Coke?" he asked.

He was grinning at me and looking crooked, the way I'd seen boys look when there are a gang of them together. I hated it, hated that grin. My heart turned over when I thought of how serious Hugh could be, how seriously he would ask me to have coffee with him, not kicking up the dust and shaking his head like a rooster, like Frank Wilson, for the whole barnyard to see and admire.

"I have to go home," I said. Frank looked as angry as I felt. For a minute, I was tempted to change my mind, to walk into the Mill, where Hugh would see me with a friend of my own. I remembered how he had jeered at Frank, and I knew he would jeer at both of us.

All Frank had done was to ask me for a Coke and call me Vicky. He couldn't know I hated that nickname. We hadn't exchanged more than twenty words in a year, yet here we were glaring at each other like mortal enemies.

"I have a lot of homework, Frank," I said, trying to sound friendly, but not too friendly. He shrugged and turned away. I wished again I'd taken him up on his offer. I walked to Autumn Street, wondering how I could find my way home and carry books when I felt I was being pulled apart like taffy. But my feet carried me. My feet didn't have thoughts. At least, I hoped they didn't.

We went to Boston for the weekend. Ma had to find out about equivalency tests and a refresher course in organic chemistry for her nursing career. I spent most of the time with Uncle Philip during the days. Lawrence came to supper both nights we were there. I noticed how every time he caught me staring at him, he'd look quickly away. I felt as though I was winning a peculiar contest. Yet I didn't feel like a winner.

I spent all of Saturday with Uncle Philip in his shop and watched customers. Some people made a beeline for a certain bolt of cloth, and you would have thought from their intent expressions that they were deciding their fates. Other people walked around dreamily, touching this piece of cloth or that, and then left without buying anything.

When we walked home at the end of the day, Uncle Philip kept my arm under his. He was holding it too tightly—I wanted to pull away from him. These days, grownups seemed dense and heavy to me, and when they began to talk to me, even Ma, I couldn't help sighing, because I wanted to get away from them—even if what they were saying was interesting.

"What's on your mind?" Uncle Philip asked. "Did you ever find your country? Remember the dream you had? About the crown of pears? I have the feeling you're not very cheery these days."

It would be simple to say I had a cold coming on. It would be impossible to explain why I was so bothered. How does everyone walk around and go about their lives with all these complicated things going on in their head? Perhaps I was especially confused. Not everybody goes to pieces when they can't find a left shoe the way I had in Jed's old room this morning. I had opened my mouth and simply howled silently until I found the shoe underneath the piled-up bedclothes.

"Tory?" Uncle Philip waited. "It's not like you to be so silent," he said. Then he spoke softly into my ear. "Can I help? Sometimes just talking—"

"Why can't things be simple!" I burst out. "Why is everything so snarled up?"

He held my arm tighter, but he didn't say a word. We walked into the hall of his apartment, and he threw his beret up on the closet shelf. "Some things are simple—or simpler than others," he said.

"Like what?" I asked. "A fried egg?"

"Even a fried egg isn't so simple when you really try to understand it," he said. "I wonder if you mean clear, not misty and uncertain? Is that what you mean?"

"I don't know," I said miserably.

Uncle Philip leaned forward and kissed my forehead.

"I hope that's clear," he said.

After supper, I sat at Jed's desk. It was too small and my knees bumped up against it. I opened my French grammar book. *S'asseoir*, I read. I took up my pen and began the conjugation. I suddenly realized my jaw was clenched. But gradually, and for the first time, as far as I can remember, I found that I liked doing my homework. What I had to do was simple—and clear. It was not trying to understand a face full of hidden thoughts and feelings; it was plain, and I knew just what I had to do.

❧ CHAPTER EIGHT

LAWRENCE HAD a lot of paper work to do, so Ma and I took the bus home Sunday afternoon. I found a note that had been slipped under our door. It was from Hugh.

"Dear Finch," it began. A new name!

Here's the solution. Let the father's death come in the second act. You'll have to write a whole new first act, poor girl! And if you insist on keeping the mother in the play, make her have a violent fight with the father and that will make her reaction more interesting when she hears of his death. How about December 20 as a deadline? I watched you go into the cemetery and sit beneath a tree, Bird, the day we did the Marx Brothers. What were you dreaming about all by yourself there? Do you like old tombstones? I do.

"Shut the door, Tory. That's a cold wind blowing. Tory? What's the matter? You look stricken!"

I sat down right then and began to tell Ma about the play. Every time she tried to ask me a question, I just raised my voice. As I went along like an express train, I discovered that by talking about one part of what troubles you, you can drown out the other part. I told Ma the Drama Club was counting on me—what a lie! I told her I didn't know how to go about changing what I'd written, or adding anything on to it. I said I wanted to get out of the whole thing but didn't know how. When my voice stopped, I could hear its echo ringing through the little house. Why had I been shouting?

"Let's go to the kitchen and make scrambled eggs and toast for supper," Ma said. I followed her, dazed by the tale that I'd patched together with bits of truth. I felt locked into a trouble that had no way out.

I stood guard over the toaster, which sometimes burned up a slice of bread in a minute, and I watched Ma beat up eggs, knowing she'd think of a way—she always had.

After the table was set, we sat down and Ma began to talk.

"Years ago," she said, "before I met Papa, I had a friend named Zachary, called Zack. His father was a union official and he was a nice man. He had a terrible failing. He gambled on everything, cards, horses, sports. He finally lost his job because of his gambling, and the family had no savings, just a little house in a Boston suburb, and that had a stiff mortgage on it. All the kids had to go to work and Zack, who was the oldest, had to leave college and find a job. They had so little money to spare that Zack had to walk into Boston if he couldn't hitch a ride. He allowed himself $1.50 for a bus ride home at the end of the day, and for lunch. That meant he could have a hot dog and a cup of coffee. Zack smoked cigars. He loved cigars. On the day I'm telling you about, he couldn't get a ride, and so he walked to the business section of the city. He hadn't had a cigar in weeks. As he was walking, he began to dream about a good job and a paycheck. He imagined himself cashing the check, walking into a tobacco store and buying two really fine cigars. He was so caught up, he didn't notice the distance he was covering. He was no longer a young man with a gambling father and no money. He was Zachary, the connoisseur of fine tobacco! At some point, he saw a tobacco store. He walked into it, bought two sixty-cent cigars, went back to the sidewalk, lit one of them, and with the first puff, the dream burst. There he was with two expensive cigars and thirty cents. When he told me about it, he was still amazed he could have imagined himself right into that real store where he had handed over his real money."

"Did he get a job?" I asked.

"Eventually. But not that day."

"He must have been furious with himself."

"He was."

"Does all that have something to do with me?"

"In a way."

She cut us pieces of leftover carrot cake and made herself a cup of coffee.

"Speaking of cigars—" she said. "I could use one myself." She looked at me. "But I won't."

"What has it got to do with me?"

"Have you spoken to Mr. Tate about Hugh's intention to use your play? Has the principal, or any other people in charge of the graduation program, accepted the idea?"

"Well—not really. Hugh just said Mr. Tate could help me with the play—"

"Have you actually talked to Mr. Tate?"

"No," I answered.

"Tory, you'd better get out of the tobacco store."

"Hugh thinks—"

"It's Hugh's dream, not yours, and from what you've told me, it's not anyone else's either."

"It's real to him," I said.

"Perhaps it is. But he can't make it come true with a playwright who doesn't want to be a playwright. I know how much you like him. I think you went along with him because you were afraid he wouldn't like you if you didn't."

I groaned out loud.

"Do you remember how, after I took you to a concert when you were around eight years old, you found an old evening gown in the attic trunk and you dressed up in it, and when I walked into the living room, there you were, standing by the piano, bowing to an invisible audience? Remember that?"

"I was little then," I said.

"Anybody, any age, can have daydreams. You know, you did have piano lessons—for a month. You hated them. What you liked was the bowing."

"Maybe I should have taken up the oboe," I said.

I felt cheerful then, while we were doing the dishes, and afterward, when we both read in the living room. I felt cheerful until I turned out my bedside lamp. Then I fell down a bottomless hole, my stomach preceding me by several feet. I couldn't speak to Mr. Tate yet. That would be real, all too real. It would end everything. I knew I was clutching at something—hanging on to a thing I couldn't see. I tried different names for it—disappointment, embarrassment, anger. Just before I fell asleep, I knew what it was. Hope. Hope that Hugh had only forgotten me for a little while at the Drama Club meeting, that he had just been businesslike, practical. Hope that everything was still as it had been, that Hugh didn't care about Tom Kyle except for Tom's interest in the Drama Club, that once things were cleared up, we would be as we had been—special friends.

I glimpsed Hugh in the hall in school, and Lucille Groome snaking along, and Tom in his ever-new clothes. Thoughts about them went around in my mind like a hamster's turning wheel. Although I did my schoolwork and my chores at home and helped Ma with the shopping and talked to people at school, I felt frozen and breakable.

One dawn, I woke up and found my blankets all over the floor. I got up and started to clean my room. I stubbed my toes on books and boxes, and I dropped things as soon as I picked them up. I realized there were tears on my face. I hadn't known I was crying. I went and crawled into my wardrobe and curled up like Ma had that time I caught her smoking. I cried until I heard my alarm clock go off. I unwound myself and got dressed. When Papa died, I knew why I was suffering. I hadn't known you could suffer without knowing the reason for it.

Frank Wilson passed me at the entrance to school without a word or a look. That irritated me, and I had an impulse to try to get his interest. The impulse lasted only until I got to my locker. I yanked open the little rusted metal door, and a note from Hugh fell on the floor.

"I miss you," it said. "I'm thinking about you even though you think I'm not."

A drawing was enclosed with the note, and he had printed a title under it. It read: *Absence makes the heart grow apples.* At first, it looked like a doodle. Then I made out a lopsided heart with two little trees growing out of it, and each tree had one apple hanging from a crooked branch.

I wanted to shout with happiness. I forgot how only a few hours earlier I'd been sobbing in my wardrobe. Everything was all right. I'd been making up the wrong daydream, like Ma's friend, Zack. I was so happy, I failed a

French quiz from thinking about how happy I was and not how irregular French verbs are.

In the afternoon, I tried to write a new scene. I finished two pages. They were awful. Nothing had changed. Nothing would change until I spoke to Mr. Tate.

I saw Mr. Tate four days every week. I was always the last student to leave the class. That was because each time I'd make up my mind to speak to him, I'd change it when he looked at me.

Why was I so afraid of something that had already happened?

I was relieved that we were reading short stories now, not plays, and that our assignments were ordinary, like writing the biography of an imaginary relative, or a comparison of three of the characters we had read about.

I hadn't realized it was almost Thanksgiving until I nearly knocked over two little kids from the first grade who were carrying papier-mâché turkey down the hall.

It was a year since Papa had died. I asked Ma what we were going to do about Thanksgiving. She answered me very carefully, as though she were afraid she would drop her words on the floor. Lawrence and Uncle Philip and Jed were coming to spend the day with us. I didn't want anyone to come, but in the end I was glad they all did. Getting dinner was hard work and I didn't have time to think about much.

The exact day came. Neither Ma nor I spoke about Papa at first. I had a strange, deep feeling of embarrassment. In the late afternoon, we went for a walk, and we hardly spoke. On the way home, I said I wanted to go to the cemetery behind the Congregational Church. When we got there, I showed Ma Letitia Cass's tombstone.

"Maybe it's better if people are buried in the ground," she said. "Then you have a place where you can visit them."

"Can you read the Latin?" I asked.

"My Latin is pretty rusty," she said. She stooped down and ran her fingers over the letters engraved on the stone. I looked down at her, and I wanted to hold on to her forever.

"Little soul . . . where will you find a home . . . poor, naked little soul, without your old power of joking . . ." she said slowly. "I think it goes something like that." She stood up next to me. "I believe that's what the Emperor Hadrian was supposed to have said on his deathbed."

We went home and had a supper of leftover turkey, and Ma finally began to speak of Papa, telling me how they had met, and how they had married, and all the places they had lived. I had heard those stories before, but I was glad to hear them again.

"Do you want the turkey wishbone?" she asked me, holding it out.

I shook my head, and she smiled at me and threw the wishbone away.

Elizabeth came to spend the afternoon with me the next Monday. We stopped in the bakery and bought sugar doughnuts and ate them on the way home, the wind blowing the crumbs behind us as we walked. The sky looked full of snow it couldn't let go of.

Elizabeth said hello to Ma, then walked right into my room, and when I followed, she closed the door.

"I have to tell you something," she said, sitting down on my bed. "I hope you won't get mad."

I began to get mad.

"Why are you looking like that?"

"Don't tell me not to get mad," I said.

"You know, you're really hard to get along with these days . . . up and down . . . like a roller coaster."

I didn't say anything.

"Do you feel unhappy about Hugh?" she asked me gently.

"What about him?" I asked in a rough voice.

"I know you don't see much of him now."

"He's busy."

"Oh, Tory!"

I went and looked out my window. A few flakes of snow had begun to fall. It had held off a long time. The November days had been cold, so cold I had just rushed from one warm place to another without looking at the sky. Now it was coming, the first snow of winter which brought such a hush and softness to everything, which made the world look so surprising. It only made me sad.

"He's got Tom Kyle following him around now," Elizabeth said. I turned and looked at her. She was touching her curly hair, then she twisted the little amethyst ring she always wore on her finger. I looked at her cable knee socks, the neat hem of her brown skirt. I thought of the mismatched socks I was wearing, which were hidden by my blue jeans.

"Why shouldn't Tom Kyle follow him around?" I asked stiffly. "I followed him around. Maybe there are things about him that you don't know. Maybe he isn't just a greedy little rat! Maybe he's different." My throat seemed to be closing up. "Maybe he's interesting!" I gasped. Then I turned my back to her and watched the big snowflakes sliding down the pane. Tom Kyle! I had hated him at first. I had wished savage, cruel things to happen to him. But I didn't hate him any more. When I saw him bending over the drinking fountain in school, bending so carefully as though he were afraid he would wrinkle, it wasn't hatred I felt. It wasn't that he looked pathetic, more like he didn't belong anywhere. It was difficult to hate someone who looked the way you felt.

"I guess I've been unfair about Hugh," Elizabeth was saying. "I'm sorry. I don't want to be mean to you. That's why I wanted to tell you I went to a movie with Frank Wilson."

"Why would you want to tell me that?"

"I mean—I went out with Frank. And I'm going out with him again."

"That's nice."

139

"You used to say you couldn't stand him."

"That's nice, too."

"Oh, Tory!" she exclaimed for the second time.

Something in me unclenched and I felt slack and indifferent. So I smiled. "Really, you don't have to apologize or explain to me," I said.

"I'll be fifteen in a few months," she said.

I burst into laughter. "Congratulations!" I said. She laughed a little, and we went out of my room and drank some cocoa and talked about school and skiing and Mr. Mellers, whose beard now covered most of his face, so he seemed to be looking out of a thicket. Finally she went home.

Ma had gone out. I sat and stared at Elizabeth's empty cup. I didn't care about Frank, yet I felt deserted. Hugh had dropped me, Elizabeth and Frank had taken each other up, and I was just hanging around, waiting.

I went to school feeling determined and grim and lonely; there was some comfort in the work I had to do. It was like a wall behind my back, something to lean on. Elizabeth and I saw each other and went sleigh riding together and she let me borrow her skis. We didn't speak of Frank or Hugh. Even though we still had fun together, a kind of nervous fun, there were moments of silence between us that were painful. I couldn't ask her about Frank Wilson. If it had been someone else she was interested in, I knew I would have asked her everything. When a certain distant look came over her face, I would know she was mooning over Frank, and then I would just want to get away from her.

The meeting of the Drama Club was getting closer. But I didn't do anything, just let it slide. Nothing seemed important.

Hugh came up to me in the hall one day and asked me to meet him at the Mill. My heart didn't lift any more than it does when I have to go to the dentist.

As I walked down the hill, every sound was clear as a bell. I heard the chains on car tires clanking on the icy street. New Oxford was covered with snow, its roofs and trees and yards, and there was ice along the edges of the Matcha River. The Mill was crowded. If I hadn't been feeling the way I was, it might have looked cozy and sweet to me—people coming in there for a little warmth and something hot to drink on a cold winter's day in a New England village that looked like a picture on a calendar. Hugh was already there, waiting for me in a booth.

He stood up as I slid into my seat. I felt suddenly shy and I didn't even say hello, just sat there.

"Take off your snowsuit, Bird," he said.

"I can't do what you want," I said. "I've tried. You'll have to find a real play."

He reached across the table and pulled my mittens off my hands. I let him. We both looked at my hands for a minute. I didn't try to hide them. Then I folded them together and looked straight at him. It seemed a very long time since I had last seen him. There were the beginnings of sideburns growing on his cheeks.

"Your play is real," he said softly. "I'm going to help you with it."

The waitress was standing next to the table looking coldly at Hugh.

"What would you like, Victoria?" he asked me.

I shook my head. He ordered coffee. The waitress sighed and went away. He smiled at me steadily, and I turned my head so as not to see that smile, which seemed to me like the glare off a surface of ice.

"You're sulking," he said at last. "Come on! You're not a sulker."

"I don't know what I am," I said. "And neither do you."

He laughed at that. I thought of how I once was so pleased by his laughter.

"I've missed you," he said.

How was he able to make it seem that it was my fault he had stopped looking for me?

"It's going to be fine, Birdie," he said. "You're feeling a little discouraged. It happens to writers."

"I'm not a writer," I said.

The coffee came, and he pushed the sugar container across the table to me. "Have your daily two pounds," he said.

At that moment, the door of the Mill opened and Tom

Kyle came in and hurried over, unwrapping a scarf from around his neck.

"You're late," Hugh said sharply. I almost laughed out loud. This coffee time hadn't been, as I'd imagined, just for Hugh and me. They'd planned to see me together. And Hugh had only been filling in the time until Tom Kyle arrived.

"I couldn't help it," Tom said, sitting down next to Hugh. "I had to clean up something in the science lab—Edsey was standing over me like a vampire. God! I was going crazy! But she wouldn't let me go. Sorry."

Tweedledum and Tweedledee, I thought, looking at the two of them, and I've been their rattle. Something unfroze in me, and something else flew out of my mind—perhaps, at last, that hope that things could be different, could be the way they once were. It was easy now for me to say what I wanted to say.

"You didn't have to hurry for me," I said. "I've already told Hugh you'll have to find another play."

Tom looked at Hugh as though he was waiting for important information.

"I'm going," I said.

"Then go," said Hugh, his head bent down, one hand flat and still on the table.

Tom looked blank. As I stood and picked up my mittens, he started to fiddle with the metal napkin container. He said, "What a tacky place! This is empty again."

I walked out of the Mill without looking back.

I got to school the next morning earlier than I ever had. A few kids were already there. Seventh- or eighth-graders, breathing out vapor in the cold, their books piled up on the steps. I wondered what thoughts were hidden under their hats. The three boys stood apart, and one punched another on the arm as though in slow motion. The two girls were huddled on the steps. As I passed them, one of the girls drew off a glove and showed the other her fingernails, which were painted a dark red. They both smiled dreamily. It was an odd world.

Mr. Tate was in his classroom looking through some papers.

He looked grumpy when he saw me, and I felt a flash of sympathy for him. I knew how often I just wanted to sit by myself in my room and not have someone walk in and talk at me.

"Can I speak to you, Mr. Tate?" I asked.

"Help yourself," he said.

"I don't want my play to be used for the graduation program," I said.

"Your play? You mean those scenes you wrote last term?"

"I told Hugh Todd, so I thought I'd better tell you."

"We haven't decided yet about a play," he said.

"I thought Hugh had spoken to you . . ."

"He did say something. But I believe he intended—or, at least, I thought he'd intended—to read your scenes for an assembly, the way the Drama Club did *Spoon River Anthology* one year and *A Child's Christmas in Wales*— I believe that was several years ago. I don't think we talked about the program for graduation. In any case, the principal has to be in on that decision, and I do, too."

I was speechless.

Mr. Tate was staring at me. "Perhaps Hugh, in his enthusiasm for what you'd written, gave you the wrong impression," he said.

"No!" I cried out. "He told me it was settled!"

"He shouldn't have done that," Mr. Tate said. "Are you very disappointed?"

I wanted to shout at him that I'd been twice-fooled, and that life was so unfair! But I couldn't say that. The balloon he had pricked had been as much mine as Hugh's. I felt shriveled.

"Victoria?"

"I'm not disappointed," I croaked. "I couldn't have written a real play. I didn't even want to."

"You do good work," he said in a kind voice. "You're a good student."

I left Mr. Tate and started toward my first class. Down the hall, I saw Hugh and, right behind him, hurrying with quick little steps, Tom Kyle. Ma's friend Zack got two cigars from his daydream. But my hands were empty.

When, a week later, the day before Christmas vacation began, I saw Mr. Tate heading toward the room where the Drama Club met, I knew any question about my scenes would be answered by him. It was over. I didn't have anything more to do.

Ma told me we were going to spend a week in Boston at Uncle Philip's and I was so relieved I nearly felt happy. I didn't want to be around New Oxford for a while.

We cleaned the house from top to bottom and finished up everything in the refrigerator. We wrapped presents and packed our suitcases. Just before Lawrence was due to pick us up to drive us to Boston, I ran over to old Mr. Thames's house with a present for Benny I'd found in a store at the shopping mall. It was a furry ball full of catnip. Benny picked it up at once, and the way he gripped it with his teeth made him look like a cat Father Time. Mr. Thames said I was to have a present, too, and to pick anything I wanted from the things in his living room. I saw a bowl of glass fruit on a table. There were cherries and a plum and a small brown pear with a bright-green glass leaf. My hand went out to it, then I pulled it back and looked uncertainly at Mr. Thames.

"The fruit?" he asked. "Take whatever you like. Now, Tory, I'm so old I say what I mean. Don't be bashful!"

I put the pear on my palm.

"When we first moved to New Oxford, I had a dream about a pear just like this one," I said.

"It's a Seckel pear," Mr. Thames said. "It's good luck for you to find a thing you've dreamed about."

I thanked him, thinking to myself that there were a

few things I'd dreamed about that I wouldn't like to run into in daylight.

Ma and Lawrence talked about apartments and heating costs and when we should put our New Oxford house up for sale all the way to Boston, and I was so bored I started pulling at the threads of an old sweater I was wearing, and I nearly had it unraveled by the time we got to the outskirts of the city.

Ma turned around from the front seat and exclaimed, "Tory! What are you doing!"

"Remodeling," I said. Lawrence glanced back at me and started to laugh.

"Don't encourage her," Ma said.

I felt grim. But when Uncle Philip opened the door to his apartment, and I saw Jed standing and grinning by the Christmas tree and supper all spread out on the table, I began to feel a touch better.

On Christmas Eve, we went to a midnight church service. When I saw the choirboys, I wondered if Hugh had looked the way they did when he was their age, nine or ten, I guess, good as gold in their black gowns and surplices, holding their music in their grubby small hands. We walked home in the crisp, black night, not talking much, and the next morning, after a huge breakfast, we opened our presents. Elizabeth had given me a silver chain with a silver bird hanging from it. She must have looked in a lot of places to find such a pretty thing.

I put on the new jacket Ma had given me, and Jed and I went out and walked for miles. It was comfortable between us, almost the way it had been years ago when we played in the attic together.

After we got back, I got the anthology of poems Lawrence had given me and began to look at it. A marker fell out, and Lawrence said from the sofa, "I thought you'd like that poem, Tory." I'd lost the place. He came over and turned the pages and then said, "There." I looked at the poem. It was by Theodore Roethke, and it was called "My Papa's Waltz." I felt a little shock and I looked at Lawrence, who had gone back to the sofa and was sitting next to Ma. His glasses had slipped down his nose. He was looking at a newspaper, bending forward under a lamp. I saw there was a lot of gray in his hair. I noticed that he was holding Ma's hand in his own. She was just sitting there, looking drowsy, her eyes half closed. I looked at Jed, who was trying to take apart a puzzle of wood, and then at Uncle Philip, who was reading a cookbook Ma had given him. I felt tearful enough to melt away. Would I ever be able to hang on to a feeling for more than five minutes?

When I got into bed, I read the poem. Even though the father in it was not like mine, the feeling was. I understood that Lawrence was telling me he knew how I felt by pointing out that particular poem. Ma, who shared the guest room with me, said from the other bed, "Did you read it?"

"Yes."

"It's lovely, isn't it?"

"Yes."

"Tory. It's as hard to be grown-up as to grow up."

"I know," I said. It wasn't true. So I said, "It can't be harder."

Ma didn't speak for a moment. Then she said, "It's amazing what people can make out of this difficult life."

I turned out my light and she turned out hers. I lay in the dark thinking how Hugh would like that poem. I imagined copying it out for him and leaving it in his locker. I had never written him a note or a letter. I imagined him reading it, and then asking me to have coffee with him, and everything being the way it had been at the beginning. I fell asleep in a daydream of happiness.

It was a nice week. Jed and I went to movies and walked out on a few, and to museums, and one day Lawrence took us to lunch at an Italian restaurant and I drank a glass of Chianti, and things were very merry. One afternoon, Jed and I returned some books to the library for Uncle Philip. Jed had to look up something in a medical dictionary for his schoolwork. We spent the afternoon looking at descriptions of diseases, and by the time we got out of the library, we were shell-shocked. "We'd be dead if we had everything we think we have," I said. "Do I look like I have a fever?" Jed asked. "Just leprosy," I said. "Take an aspirin." On our last night, we all played Monopoly and I cleaned up. I was so triumphant that even Uncle

Philip got annoyed with me. "I'm glad you're not my landlord," he said.

We returned to our cold house on Sunday. Lawrence started a fire in the stove and Ma made us an early supper out of the groceries she'd bought in Boston. There were still a few days before school began. I was sorry I'd cleaned my room so well. I didn't even have any homework to do. The minute we'd driven into New Oxford, all the troubles that seemed to have gone away in Boston came flying back to me like a flock of noisy crows.

I picked up the phone and called Elizabeth.

"I love the necklace," I said.

"I loved the gloves. Green is my favorite color," she said.

I thought of Frank Wilson's green sneakers and I made a face at the phone.

"I'm glad you're back," she said. "Listen, Frank's been working on an old junk car for months and he's got it ready to run. He wants to drive up Mt. Crystal tomorrow evening. Will you come with us? I've only been up to the top in the summer. But at this time of year, you're supposed to be able to see three states and the lights of Boston if it's a clear night."

I didn't want to go at all, but I felt Elizabeth was trying to include me in her life in some way, and also, I figured I'd better hang on to whatever was left for me in New Oxford.

"I'll ask Ma," I said, "and I'll call you back in the morning."

When I went to bed and turned out the light, a ray from the street lamp struck the little glass pear on my bureau, which old Mr. Thames had given me. I remembered Uncle Philip telling me that my pear dream meant I'd have to find my own country. If I had, I thought, most of the population had fled from it.

CHAPTER NINE

IT SHOULD HAVE BEEN a straightforward question, but when I asked Ma if I could go for a ride with Frank and Elizabeth, I heard my voice and it was wheedling and slick and not straightforward at all. Ma suddenly darted off to the kitchen, saying she'd left something on the stove, and when she came back she was frowning, and she asked me what I had asked her as though it had been a year ago. Why was she being so difficult? I described Frank's car —which I had not seen—and told her what good friends Elizabeth and Frank were. The more I talked, the falser I sounded. Ma was sitting on the sofa, staring at the stove. I went and stood in front of it. Finally, she looked up at me. Her expression was puzzled, but all she said was, "Tory, you can go, but be home by ten." I grabbed the phone and called Elizabeth. "Why are you whispering?" she asked. I shouted that I'd meet her in ten minutes. Then I hung up and flung on my clothes and got out in a hurry. And when the door closed behind me and I looked down the dark street and felt the cold wind and saw the shut-away, secret look of the houses, I felt on my own and alone and worried.

I was glad that I had told Elizabeth—on an impulse I hadn't given a thought to—that I'd meet them in front of the old movie house. But why? I ran nearly all the way there as though I could leave my confusion behind me on my own doorstep. I slowed down on Main Street and stared into the windows of the bakery where a sleeping cat had curled itself next to a stale-looking loaf of bread. I wished I was asleep, too.

It was fiercely cold and the usual group wasn't hanging around under the marquee. But just in front of it was a parked black car, and I could see Elizabeth and Frank sitting in the front seat. She waved at me through the windshield. My heart skipped a beat; I felt breathless as though I was riding the crest of a high wave and had, all at once, glimpsed the sliding, shifting sand far below.

As I drew close, I could smell fresh paint on the car, which looked like an antique. It was just a black box with wheels and a narrow running board. Frank reached over Elizabeth's shoulder and opened the back door, and I climbed up and in.

"Hello, Vicky," he said. Elizabeth shot him a look but said nothing. Did he call her Lizzie? I wondered. She looked very sedate, sitting there with her hands folded on her lap.

Frank turned on the ignition. "Takes a while each time," he said to no one in particular.

"There's Tom Kyle," Elizabeth said suddenly, as the car coughed and rattled.

He was standing in front of the entrance to the Mill, and the door was closing behind him. I saw him look up and down the street, then wrap his long scarf around his neck. He stamped one foot, then the other, stared up at the sky, then, as his glance fell, he saw us. He smiled faintly in our direction, and the anger I'd seen on his face disappeared as though a hand had smoothed it away. He walked slowly toward us and Elizabeth cranked down her window and called hello.

"Is this a car?" he asked Frank.

"Made by hand," Frank said, "every inch of it." He looked slyly at Elizabeth. "Want to come with us?" he asked. "We're going up Mt. Crystal."

It must have been owner's pride in the car that made Frank ask Tom. I couldn't believe he cared much for his company. As far as I knew, no one in the sophomore class was especially friendly to him.

Tom glanced back at the Mill. "My friend is late, very late," he said, mostly to himself. His friend. Hugh had stood him up, I guessed.

"All right, I'll come along," he said, as though persuaded against his will. He got into the back seat, next to me, and coiled his scarf on his lap. He didn't look at me at all.

"We're off," Frank said, and the car, which had been idling, jumped and began to move.

It was damp and cold inside, like the cellar of a deserted house. I sat as far away as I could from Tom. We didn't move; we didn't speak. In the front seat, Elizabeth and Frank muttered to each other, and laughed and hummed songs and paid their two silent passengers no attention at all.

I'm going to make a big scene, I thought. I'm going to ask Frank to stop the car and let me out, and when they ask me why, I'm going to say that I have better things to do with time than spend it with two idiots and one snowman. I didn't. But I felt a little better just imagining the scene. Frank asked Tom what he thought about New Oxford's basketball team and its chances against a neighboring village team. Tom replied he didn't know much about the chances because he wasn't much interested in basketball. I don't know whether he meant to be scornful, but he sounded that way, and I thought of Hugh's easy, indifferent dismissal of sports, of anything that didn't interest him.

"Yeah? Well, I'm interested, and so is everyone else," Frank said in a challenging voice, and Tom said uneasily, "I guess so."

We were out of the village now and on a blacktop road that went past several farmhouses.

"Isn't one of those houses where you live?" Elizabeth asked.

"No," Tom said, and that was all. I saw Elizabeth and Frank exchange significant glances, and I felt as if I'd been slapped, even though their silent little conversation wasn't about me but about Tom. It was as if I was the one who wasn't giving the right answers.

"Runs like a dream," Frank announced. Why did he leave out pronouns, like a television-commercial announcer?

"It's amazing," Elizabeth said, "I don't know how you did it!"

"Had to hit a dozen places to find parts," he said.

We suddenly veered sharply to the right and Elizabeth let out a small, very polite, scream. Tom was thrown against me and his elbow hit my rib cage. "Sorry," he muttered.

"A little ice," Frank said. "Notice how the wheels held?"

"Great," said Elizabeth.

Tom and I rearranged ourselves, making sure nothing touched, not our coats or our scarves or our feet on the narrow floor space. Had he been given orders by Hugh not to speak to me?

Frank turned off the road we had been following, and at once, we began to climb. Frank and Elizabeth weren't murmuring now. He was hunched over the steering wheel, working the gearshift back and forth as the road grew steeper. On our right, the dark pine forest on the slopes I had glimpsed all the way from Autumn Street rose like a vast black cliff. Ahead, on the narrow road, I saw large patches of ice shining in the headlights. Then the road would curve in a hairpin turn and we'd be driving next to the mountain itself where boulders loomed over us and seemed, as we passed them, to be only momentarily at rest, ready in an instant to tumble down and silence the rattling little car and its passengers. I began to be scared.

"It's pretty icy, isn't it?" Tom asked anxiously. He leaned forward toward the front seat. "Maybe we'd better not try it," he said. "We could take a bad skid."

Frank said nothing, only bent closer over the steering wheel.

The cold was intense and I felt it to my bare, shivering bones. There were no street lamps; we could see only the road and the pale watery headlights. What could live in that forest? Everything, I imagined, was by itself and silent —a hunting fox, a snake beneath a rock coiled in winter sleep, a bird, half frozen on a branch, strayed off its course to a warmer place. I looked at Elizabeth, and she, too, looked frozen. Tom moved and fidgeted constantly, straining to stare out the window, sinking back, then rearing up.

"Let's go back," I croaked.

"No," Frank said. It was a no like a dropped stone.

"I think—" Tom began.

"No!" Frank shouted. "We're going all the way up to the top!"

We wound upward. I saw a broken wood railing, the jagged edges pointing out toward nothing, and I wondered what had crashed through it, and I shivered and my teeth chattered. When we skidded, Frank would turn and twist the wheel violently. Each time we went into a sickening slide I felt as though I were falling into a black ravine. I heard Tom gasp. Once he made a noise like a puppy—it was such a small noise, so private, I think I was the only one to hear it.

Then there were no more trees, only a sense of the earth falling away forever. We were nearly flying. We were in a frozen tin box, attached to the earth by Frank's hands on the steering wheel. I couldn't think what Frank looked like. I told myself he had a mustache and reddish hair, but he had become for me some senseless thing that drove on.

Suddenly we stopped. We were there, on the top of the mountain. Our deep-drawn breaths sounded as though we were lowering pails into a well for water. Frank laughed.

"We did it! The car did it! Come on! Let's get out."

We were next to a parking area where people probably came in the summer to see the view. It was covered with drifts of snow, and as we walked through them, there was a sound like many candles being blown out. An iron railing circled the parking place, and when we reached it, I could see the earth far below us, a dark ocean with pools of light here and there like ships. One of those pools might have been New Oxford. Frank pointed to a haze of light at the farthest horizon. "That's Boston," he said, so proudly you would have thought he was pointing at his own city.

We were looking at a great living map. The air was

sharp and it crackled like a new bill. My lungs ached. Above us, the icy stars glittered; in the forest below, perhaps, a snowshoe rabbit was poised, listening to the echo of our racketing passage up the mountain, a sound as mysterious to it as the stars were to me. I was looking down at the world, and I felt such a wave of happiness I thought I would sail out into space.

"We'll have to go back," called Tom. I turned and saw him standing close to the car. With one hand, he clutched a door handle as though he were teetering on the edge of a cliff. "It'll be worse going back," he said.

"You don't skid any worse going down than going up," Frank said scornfully. "Why don't you take it easy?"

"Much worse," Tom said in that voice of his which didn't rise or fall, which didn't match up with the way he looked or the words he spoke. I could tell he was too frightened to take a step away from the car. Yet how strange it was that he held on to the car so desperately, held on to the thing he dreaded.

"Maybe you'd better walk down," Frank said as he stomped through the drifts toward the car. Elizabeth stepped precisely in his boot prints. Her head was down and I couldn't see her face. "Are you scared?" I asked her. "Oh, Tory," she exclaimed, not looking up. What did that mean?

Frank had already swung into the driver's seat, and Elizabeth and I were standing next to Tom.

"I will walk down," he said in a low voice.

"It's miles," I said.

"He'll kill us," he said.

Elizabeth put her hand on the car door. "He won't kill us," she said in a voice as cold as the air. "He's a good driver." She got in and sat there, letting whoever cared to look at her calm profile. I suddenly remembered her face swollen with hives. Did having a boyfriend have to make a person so proud?

"We'd better get in," I said to Tom. "You can't walk down. You'd freeze to death."

He looked at me for an instant, then he opened the door and waited while I got in. I was thinking hard about the expression I had seen on his face and I forgot for a moment what might lie ahead of us. He had looked timid. Tom Kyle was timid. Did Hugh tell him what was important and what wasn't? Did he tell him what to do, the way he used to tell me what to do? I looked sideways at Tom. He was huddled in the corner of the seat, that long scarf wrapped around the lower part of his face. I wanted to say something to him—I don't know what. I wanted him to speak to me.

Frank started the car. It coughed and shook and he drove it in a circle until it was facing downhill.

"Okay," he said. "Here we go."

Everything was fine for a few minutes. Then we lurched forward and slipped sideways to the edge of the road. Frank stamped on the brake, and Elizabeth shouted, "No brakes! My father said no brakes on ice!"

"Shut up!" Frank yelled. "Everybody shut up!" Tom

and I piled up like a football scramble. Elizabeth was flung forward against the windshield, and she screamed. Oh, my poor Ma, I thought. We'll all be dead soon! The car straightened out; the pale lights that felt along the road like an insect's antennae went off.

"Okay, okay . . ." Frank muttered. "That's the worst of it." He started up and we inched forward in first gear. Elizabeth had her hands on her head. "Are you all right?" I asked. She just shook her head. I looked at Tom, and he had his gloved hands on his face.

"I can't stand this!" I said. "Let us out!"

Frank didn't stop. We went along with no skids for a while. I noticed a large boulder I'd seen on the way up and I knew we were close to the tree line. If we have an accident now, I thought, at least the trees will stop us from tumbling down the whole mountain.

We hit ice. The car spun completely around. Tom and Elizabeth and I all screamed together as if we were singing, but Frank was silent, bent over the wheel like a demon, his elbows straight out. The engine stuttered and stopped. We were facing up the mountain. We were still alive. I heard Tom Kyle gasping into his scarf. I realized he was crying.

"Listen," Frank said weakly. We all listened. "We made it," he said. "I'll just turn around. We're nearly down. Nothing can happen now. Listen . . . we're all right."

We skittered a hundred yards or so and emerged on the main road to New Oxford. Frank was sitting up straight now, and I looked at him, my mind full of murderer's thoughts.

Elizabeth said, in a voice that trembled, "We shouldn't have gone up there."

No one spoke.

As Frank drew up and parked in front of the Mill, I saw there were a few people inside, eating and talking. That meant it wasn't ten yet, when the Mill closed. How long had we been gone? The time that clocks measured might be uniform, but there was no measurement I could think of for what had happened to us on Mt. Crystal. Should I thank Frank for the ride and then hit him? He was opening the door for Tom and me. Why didn't Tom move? Why did he just sit there?

"Are you getting out?" Frank was asking. Suddenly I saw Hugh's face just above the plastic turkey in the window of the Mill. He was standing there, looking out at us.

I touched Tom's arm, and he moved very slowly. Just as he got his feet on the sidewalk, Hugh came quickly out of the restaurant door. Tom was holding his bunched scarf in his hands. He looked dazed, as though he didn't know where he was.

"I've been waiting for you for an hour!" Hugh said in such an accusing voice I would have been only a little surprised if he'd taken out a rope, tied Tom up, and led him away.

Tom said nothing. Frank was staring at him, at his

trousers. I looked. I saw dark uneven stains like the shadows of tall grass.

"Where did you go—what were you doing with them?" Hugh shouted.

Tom's voice rose in a thin wail. "I waited for you . . ."

Hugh turned and walked away up the hill. Tom wrapped his scarf around his throat, letting one end of it hang down to hide the stains on his pants. He glanced once at Frank and said without any expression at all—as if he were talking about the weather—"You freak." Then he walked down Main Street and I watched him until he vanished from sight.

"He wet himself," Frank said. "He was scared out of his mind and he wet himself."

Elizabeth rolled down her window and stuck her head out.

"What's going on?" she asked.

"I'll drive you home, Vicky," Frank said.

"No," I stated. "You won't."

The Mill's display window went dark. Lights stayed on only at the back, where the kitchen was, and I saw the waitress lean against the wall and light a cigarette. Two men wearing similar plaid jackets stepped out the door and said good night to each other and walked off. I heard Frank sigh as he went to get in his car, and I heard Elizabeth roll up her window. They were shut away now. The street felt peculiarly empty, as though there was no life anywhere in it, only weather. The cold was suddenly unbearable. I started quickly toward home.

Our living-room lights were on, and I saw Ma bent over a book at the table in front of the windows. All at once, I knew why I'd had such trouble getting her to say I could go for a ride with Elizabeth and Frank. It wasn't what I'd said that had made her hesitate so—it was what I'd known, that it would be dangerous. It was what I concealed—that we were going to drive up the mountain. And she had heard in my voice something hidden.

"How was your ride?" she asked when I opened the door.

"Fine," I said. I walked into the kitchen, dropped the milk carton getting it out of the refrigerator, and spilled cocoa in the sink. I gave up and put both milk and cocoa away.

"Tory?" Ma called. "How was Frank's car?"

"He's a wonderful driver," I said, and I felt disgusted with myself. She couldn't know why I had spoken so mockingly. I couldn't explain anything now. "I'm tired," I said. "I'm going to bed."

In my room, I dug around until I found my old copy of *Robin Hood and His Merry Men*. I hadn't looked at it in a long time. When I was little, Papa had read it to me at night. I had loved Will Scarlet, and I had often fallen asleep imagining myself joining Robin's band in Sherwood Forest. But tonight, the printed words didn't have their old magic. It was not Will Scarlet I pictured; it was Tom Kyle and his misery.

Elizabeth phoned me in the morning. She kept saying how terrible our ride had been. Each time I would agree with her, she would say what a marvelous driver Frank was. So I stopped agreeing with her about how awful things had been, and she went on to talk about Tom.

"I couldn't see what had happened," she said, "but Frank told me."

I told her I'd seen the same thing happen to a little girl in the third grade in my old school in Boston. She was supposed to play Spontaneous Combustion in a school program about the causes of fire. "Right on the stage, in assembly," I said.

"I'd die," Elizabeth said. "I'd never get over it."

"She got over it," I said. "But it took a while."

"Well, *I'm* not going to tell anyone," Elizabeth said, as though I'd accused her.

The few days left before school started were long days for me, bound at either end by the winter dark. The winter felt like a hard shell, and I longed for it to crack, to break open. Whatever I thought of doing seemed pointless. When Ma was out, I watched television until I felt as if I'd stuffed myself with stale marshmallows. Then I'd look out the window. Then I'd eat crackers.

"Tory, wash your hair!" Ma said to me one morning. "You look like Medusa."

I wanted to look like Medusa; I wanted to wear socks that didn't match, and shirts with missing buttons. Sherwood Forest would have been much too active and well furnished for me these days. I wanted to be a bum.

But I washed my hair, and while I was standing in the shower, half dreaming of I don't know what under the streaming water, I thought about Tom and how he wasn't wonderful or special or even more interesting than I was. I thought about how I'd been when we'd moved to New Oxford, jumpy and frightened and raw, and Hugh had taken me out of all those feelings. Papa's death had made me timid. I don't know what made Tom timid. But that's how we were alike. And I realized Hugh must have liked us because we both were timid and uncertain. I hadn't ever thought before that you could be liked for your shortcomings.

I knew that Hugh would drop Tom, just as he'd dropped me. He had to be the only person in your life—and when he thought he wasn't, he'd desert you. If he once saw you as ridiculous, he'd turn away from you forever. How would he ever find a human being who wasn't ridiculous sometimes?

On New Year's Eve, Ma and I stayed up until midnight. I heard one faint horn note somewhere at the end of Autumn Street right after the church bells rang in the year. It made us both laugh.

"Old Mr. Thames," said Ma.

"More likely Benny," I said.

I lay awake a long time after midnight, wondering what was going to happen in the next twelve months.

On January 3, I went back to school, and the first person I saw going up the path was Hugh. I waited until he went in.

I didn't see him again for a week, and then it was at a distance, as he walked partway down the hill toward his house. In that week, everyone heard about Tom Kyle. The kindest way I heard the story told was by a girl in my French class, who said, "I hear there was an accident *in* Frank Wilson's car, not out of it!"

I told her that if she'd been there, the same thing might have happened to her, that we'd nearly got killed. But she only laughed. What can you do against that kind of laugh? It threw a person right out of the world.

I heard the Drama Club had decided on a play for graduation, so I asked Mr. Tate about it and he told me they were going to do *The Mikado*. Even though I didn't want to know much about it, I asked him if everyone had agreed to that—Hugh? Lucille? Tom Kyle? He said Tom Kyle had resigned from the club saying he had too much to do, catching up on work he'd missed because of transferring from another school.

I saw Tom in the hall once, and on an impulse, I went over to speak to him. But he gave me such a terrible look I backed up and banged into the wall.

"I didn't tell anyone," Elizabeth said, even though I hadn't asked her. "I guess you didn't. And I know Frank wouldn't."

Was she lying to me? I couldn't bear the thought of it. When people you like lie to you, you crumple.

"I bet it was Hugh," she said. "He was there. He must have seen what happened."

All I said was that maybe Hugh hadn't seen.

I told myself that Frank must have told someone. There was no point in saying that to Elizabeth. She said it would all blow over anyhow, and we both smiled falsely and dropped the subject.

I felt so alone. Last year I'd been taken up with Hugh and I hadn't paid attention to the other kids in the school. Now they didn't pay much attention to me. For the first time, I was glad we were going to move back to Boston in June. I wanted to start all over again in another place. I felt the way I sometimes do about my room, when it's such a horror there doesn't seem to be anything to do except move out of it entirely and lock the door.

Ma spent quite a few days every week in Boston, taking her refresher courses. Also, she and Lawrence were still looking for a place for us to live. Pretty soon, she said, we'd have to put our house up for sale.

There was a mild springlike day toward the end of January, and I got on my bicycle and rode to a town four miles from New Oxford where there was a beauty parlor. I had my hair cut.

When I looked at myself later in the little Mexican mirror Elizabeth had given me, I hardly recognized myself.

"It looks good," Ma said. "What made you decide to cut it?"

I couldn't answer. I didn't know.

By that time, jokes about the "accident" in Frank's car had died down. I saw that people forget even the worst things about other people. I suppose it's because their own lives gallop ahead and they have enough to think about just trying to stay upright.

Elizabeth told me that Frank had told her Tom was absent from school a good deal these days. I didn't even feel like guessing about Tom and his troubles. Hugh and I passed each other in the halls without a look, without one word.

How could that be? How could people never speak again? How could I not speak to Hugh Todd? And it was all I could do—not to speak to him, even if it was to say just one word—hello. Despite all that had happened, I wanted to break out of our silence. It smothered me like a sweater you can't pull down because the neck is too tight, and I felt caught, and breathless, flailing around, trying to rip the sweater off.

How could people who had spoken so privately to each other for so long behave as if they'd never known each other? Our silence was a kind of terrible lying. That's what it was. It shamed me more than anything ever had.

Each day as I walked home and came to the crest of the

hill where one road turned off toward Hugh's house I'd think about that silence. One day in English, we had to write down what our idea of happiness was. I scribbled down something about a late-afternoon picnic at the beach, but when I passed Hugh's road that afternoon, I knew what my real idea of happiness was. It was feeling the way I had once felt toward Hugh. I had been happy then, I thought, without knowing it.

The truth was that I didn't miss Hugh any more. I missed, terribly, the way I had felt about him.

CHAPTER TEN

THERE WAS A BLIZZARD during the last week of January and school closed for a week.

After the snow had stopped, there were perfect clear days, the spiny shadows of the bare trees falling across the snow, and plumes of smoke rising straight up from the fireplaces and stoves of New Oxford, and all around the village the smooth glittering fields of winter. Every house looked inviting.

The snowplows were everywhere, pushing away the great heaps of snow from the roads. People rode their sleighs and skied down Main Street. Frank got work helping the snow-clearing crews and so I saw more of Elizabeth than I had for a while. She wouldn't eat sugar doughnuts any more. She said she was afraid of gaining weight. So I ate them by myself, and I took a contrary pleasure in her disgusted looks.

One afternoon, she and I went to the Mill. As we walked

by the movie house, freshly boarded up, Elizabeth told me some boys had broken into it the night before and had drunk up several gallons of wine, and two of them had gotten sick enough to have to go to the hospital. A lot of things were always going on, even in a little village like New Oxford, and you always heard about them sooner or later.

We had grilled cheese sandwiches and hot chocolate, and it felt like old times. Elizabeth told me she was thinking of going to music school when she finished high school. Her face had a certain seriousness when she talked about the cello. I loved that. I told her I wished I, too, knew how to do something well, something not connected with ordinary school. At that moment, Frank Wilson burst into the restaurant, came over to us, and sat down next to Elizabeth. His reddish mustache was like a stroke of red crayon against the paleness of his skin.

Elizabeth smiled in that new cozy secret way of hers and I wanted to pinch her.

"Frank?"

"Tom Kyle's been in a car accident on Mt. Crystal," he said.

Elizabeth pushed her plate away violently and it slid across the table. I caught it just before it fell. My chest had tightened so I could hardly draw a breath.

"Is he dead?" asked Elizabeth.

"Not yet," Frank said. "The car he was driving was wedged between two rocks and they stopped it from rolling all the way down. One of the guys on the crew spotted the car when we were working on the road going to the mountain. They took him to the hospital in Regency."

"Did you see him?" I asked.

"From a distance. When they pulled him out of the car."

"I want to go home," Elizabeth said.

But we sat there, not speaking, until, minutes later, Elizabeth took a dollar from her change purse and handed it to me. "Tory, will you—?" she began, then seemed to give up saying anything more. Frank took her hand and she stood and they both left, their arms around each other. The waitress padded over and I asked her for the check, paid, and went out into the cold.

At home, I lay on my bed staring up at the ceiling until Ma came to stand in the doorway.

"Tory?" she asked softly.

I told her. When I said that Tom had whimpered like a puppy, she put her hands over her face, and when I described how he had tried to hide his wetness with his scarf, she cried, "Such an ordinary, human thing to happen to a person!" After I had finished with Frank's news at the Mill, she came over and sat on the bed and looked into my face. I thought I could read in hers the grief she would have felt if something had happened to me in Frank's car that night on Mt. Crystal. She didn't reproach me; she didn't have to.

She got up and went to the phone and I heard her

asking the operator for the number of the Regency hospital. When she came back to my room, she said, "Critical."

Later, Elizabeth called. Frank had heard that Tom had been taken by ambulance from Regency to a Boston hospital. "He's broken like a smashed cup," she said. "His ribs, his right leg, his left arm."

I was afraid to go to school Monday for fear of what I would hear. There were only a few bits of information, and they were repeated over and over again. Tom's father had taken the bus to Boston. Tom's mother had seen Tom shoveling the snow from their driveway, then had seen him back out the car. She had thought he was driving into New Oxford. He was going to be in the hospital a long time. That was all.

Ma phoned the Kyles that evening, and she spoke to Mr. Kyle, who thanked her for calling and said they were managing, and Tom's condition was "uncertain"—he would live but they didn't know how damaged he would be—and he couldn't understand what had possessed Tom to drive up that mountain road before the road crews had gotten to it.

I knew what had possessed him. Humiliation.

After a while, nobody in school had talked about what had happened to Tom in Frank's car that night. It had kept on happening for Tom.

During the next few days, I saw how people make their feelings into thoughts, then turn those thoughts into facts that seem to have always been there. I met Frank outside the library, where he was waiting for Elizabeth to return some books.

"I've been thinking about the accident," he said, "thinking about Tom Kyle going up there again to the mountain." His tone was confiding, as if he and I'd been friends for years. I didn't want to talk about Tom with Frank and I started to move on.

"Wait a minute, Vicky. I know what happened. See, Tom would have got over all that—it was Hugh Todd who drove him to go back. Todd would've driven him crazy, probably. That's what he's like, Hugh, always has been mean, a lousy friend—that's why he *hasn't* a friend. A nasty little snot like that."

"You don't know that. You don't know if Hugh ever said a word about it to Tom," I said.

"He's always been rotten to everyone, above the rest of us," Frank said angrily. "It had to be the way I said."

I left him standing there, all smug and wrapped up in what he knew.

But in a couple of days, the kids in school I talked to were saying that what had happened to Tom was Hugh's fault. Nobody was saying "probably" any more. Hugh had tormented Tom, teased him into trying to drive up Mt. Crystal. So Frank's "facts" became the way people understood Tom's accident. I told everyone who spoke to me about it how Frank wouldn't turn back that night, even though Tom and I had begged him to. No one paid any attention. They seemed to have heard the story they wanted to hear, and nothing else they heard was going to change their minds. I hated the snarl of it all; I hated the way no one had any doubts, especially Frank Wilson. It wasn't even that I wanted to defend Hugh. I didn't like being a part of the gossip snowball that was gathering up debris as it rolled faster and faster through the school.

I kept imagining Tom, alone in that car, half dead in the morning silence on the mountain slope. Whose fault had it been? If Hugh hadn't been late getting to the Mill, Tom wouldn't have come with us. Why was being afraid such a terrible, disgusting thing? Wasn't everybody afraid sometimes? But why had Hugh turned his back on Tom and walked away from him because Tom had been with us? Did Hugh make anyone he paid attention to into a tightrope walker? Hadn't I been one, too, with Hugh?

One morning that week, all classes went to the auditorium to see a movie about condors and to hear a talk about them by a Boston ornithologist. Each class filed in and sat down in designated rows. The last to come in were the seniors. Hugh led one line of students into a row and sat down. Instead of sitting next to him, the next boy in line left an empty seat between himself and Hugh. The teacher pointed to the empty seat but the boy refused to take it. Hugh sat as unmoving as a statue. I could see a flush begin at his neck and flood upward like something he was drowning in. Finally, the teacher took the empty seat herself. People had been mad at Hugh for years, mad at him for the kind of person he was. Now they thought they had something on him—something they could really blame him for.

Ma and I went to Boston the next weekend. Lawrence had finally found an apartment and we were to go and look at it. It was the top floor of a big, old stone house. Ma said I could have the room with the fireplace. It didn't work, but it looked pretty. There were light areas on the dirty blue walls where the former tenants must have hung their pictures. Where had they gone? I felt sad and droopy, and I could see that Ma and Lawrence were disappointed. I suppose they'd hoped I would be enthusiastic. I couldn't even pretend.

On Saturday, I went with Uncle Philip to his store, where I hung around for a while. Then I told him I was going for a walk. The sky was gray, the snow in Boston dirty and crusted with garbage. I walked very slowly until I came to the hospital where Tom was. I almost turned back. I hated hospitals. Suddenly I just flung myself through the doors.

At the information desk, they told me visiting hours didn't begin for another hour and that I could stay only fifteen minutes with the patient I'd come to see. I sat in the lobby watching people come and go, thinking about what was behind the rubber-edged doors that swung back and forth silently as nurses and orderlies went through them. I saw a woman step out of an elevator carrying a new baby wrapped up in a yellow blanket. A man was holding her elbow and clutching a bouquet of faded flowers. The woman's skin was rosy and she looked eager, as if she were going to a party. I was glad that not everyone was sick in the hospital.

It was time. When I got to Tom's floor, I nearly turned back again to the elevator. There was something about those waxed gray floors that frightened me even more than the half-opened doors of the rooms.

I paused outside Tom's room. I could see a television set suspended from the ceiling. I walked in. Tom was next to the window. The other bed was disordered but empty. One of Tom's legs hung in traction, and one of his arms was held rigid between two boards. Tubes snaked out from under the white coverlet and connected up with a machine near the head of the bed. On the little bedside table was a glass with a glass straw in it that curved at the top. A small radio next to it was playing softly.

Tom's face and head were not bandaged, but everything else I could see was. He was staring at the window.

"Tom?" I whispered from the foot of his bed.

He turned his head slowly. His face looked very small, as though it had shrunk, and his sideburns were gone. I saw his eyes widen.

"Tory," he said in a low hoarse voice like a radio full of static.

I knew it was a ridiculous question, but I asked it. "How are you?"

"Great," he croaked.

A nurse came in at that moment carrying a small tray.

I saw Tom flinch. All that was on the tray was a tiny fluted cup. There must have been other trays—with awful things on them.

"A little pill for a little pill," said the nurse gaily, and she pushed back his hair from his forehead. "Let's see you swallow this." He opened his mouth the way a bird opens its beak. She held the glass with the curved straw to his lips. When she left, Tom looked at a chair in the corner near the window. "Sit down," he said, "if you want to."

I kept my hands on the iron frame of the bed and just stood there. He didn't ask me to sit down again.

"My leg is going to be okay," he said. "But they have to do another operation on my arm." He closed his eyes for a minute. "You're the only person from school who's come to see me," he said. "The sophomore class sent me a card." He smiled slightly. "It told me to get well soon."

"Will you?" I asked.

"I don't know," he replied.

I went and sat down in the chair, and he followed me with his eyes. "Pop comes and has lunch with me," he said. "And my sisters."

"I didn't know you had sisters," I said, surprised.

"They're much older than me. One is married."

"In my family, there's only me and Ma, and my Uncle Philip and his son," I said.

He didn't say anything for a bit. He seemed asleep. Then he opened his eyes and said, "Some people know how to drive right off. People like Frank Wilson. It's like they

179

were born in a car." It took him a long time to say that. He seemed to have trouble breathing. "They thought I was dead when they found me. I could hear them saying I was dead."

"They were wrong!" I exclaimed, my voice shooting up. An old man shuffled into the room, glanced over at us, and then went to sit on the other bed with his back to us. He began to fuss with a box of Kleenex.

"Why did you go back up there?" I asked.

"*You* know . . ." Tom said.

"But we were all so scared that night."

"Not the way I was."

There was a long silence then. Finally, he spoke again.

"I may be able to get up in a few weeks."

I had the feeling I'd stayed as long as I should. I went to the side of Tom's bed.

"I'm sorry you had the accident," I said.

"Me, too," he answered.

Then I touched his cheek with a finger. I had never touched a boy's cheek before, and when I had imagined doing it, as I had, it had not been Tom's cheek.

"Thank you for coming to see me," he said.

I didn't tell anyone I had gone to see Tom, not Ma, not Elizabeth. It was my secret, and I kept it to myself.

In February, Hugh resigned from the Drama Club, and a week later he left school for good. No one knew where he had gone, and they didn't seem interested enough to try and guess. I felt a kind of last desperation about him and so I asked Mr. Tate. He'd heard that Hugh was being tutored in Boston and would take some kind of equivalency test to graduate, and that was all. Mrs. O'Connor, our neighbor, told Ma the Todds had sold their house on the Matcha River, but old Mr. Thames said the Todds never let go of anything permanently and they had probably only rented it.

We heard Tom Kyle was walking, but his left arm had not healed and he had to have more operations on it.

In April, a young couple with a baby put down a deposit on our house. We were to move to the new apartment in June, right after Ma and Lawrence were married. Lawrence was already living in the apartment, having everything painted and nailed up and tacked down.

Spring came early. I walked out of school one day into the damp sweetness of the air and I suddenly felt like yelling at the top of my lungs, yelling that the snow was gone—the cold, gray days gone. I sang silently to myself as I walked toward the crest of the hill, where the road divided into two roads, one going down Main Street, the other in the direction of Hugh's house. I wanted to see it suddenly. Suddenly I had to go there.

I passed the long driveways that led to the homes hidden by evergreens. The Matcha was in full flood and roaring like lions. Everything else was silent, and as I neared his house, the silence crept into me.

There was a car parked in front of it, the trunk open. I looked up at the windows. I was about to turn away when I realized someone was looking down at me. It was Mrs. Howarth, Hugh's mother. She was wearing a fur hat, and she waved a gloved hand at me. I waved back, then started back down the drive. I heard the window open, then her voice calling, "Wait!"

In a minute, she had opened the front door and was standing there in a long tweed coat of many colors.

"Come in," she said. "You're Victoria, aren't you? Hugh's friend who plays the oboe?"

I stepped inside. There was no furniture in the hall, no rugs, and none in the rooms I could see through half-opened doors. There were only two boxes on the floor, piled high with papers.

"We've sold the house," she said. "I had to come back to check on things. Broom-clean, they say in the bill of sale. So I've just been gathering up a few bits of things we forgot."

She spoke quickly as though she were on the steps of a train about to leave, and she smiled at me all the time.

"How is Hugh?" I asked.

"Wonderful," she said. "He's wonderful." She began to fiddle with her gloves, pulling them half off, then putting them back on. "He's very gifted, you know, very imaginative. But then you must know. You were his friend, weren't you?"

I said yes and looked down at the box near my feet. In it, there were several books, a few objects wrapped in newspaper, and loose papers. One of the papers had a drawing on it. I leaned over to see it better, aware of Mrs.

Howarth's stare. It was a drawing of a small boy wearing a peaked hat. He was holding a curling string that was attached to a red kite in the sky.

I looked at her. "Well—goodbye," I said.

She nodded. I'd almost turned away when I said, "Can I help you put the boxes in your car?"

"No, no . . ." she answered. "Mr. Howarth is upstairs taking a final look around. He will do that. But, thank you, Victoria."

"I don't really play the oboe," I said.

"Oh?" she said politely. "Hugh was mistaken, then."

I walked back to Main Street. Hugh must not even have remembered that the story his father had drawn for him that rainy night was about a little boy and a kite. Yet even though he'd forgotten, the memory had come back in another way. Perhaps there was no forgetting—memory just returned in new shapes. Perhaps, years from now, I'd try on an old tweed hat and I'd feel something mysterious, and I'd laugh at myself and not even know I was thinking about my father.

How would Tom Kyle remember Hugh? What had they talked about together? Or had Tom just listened, wanting to learn a different way to be, the way I had, and letting Hugh fill up the space around him the way he had filled it up for me? And, perhaps, filling up the empty space in himself. Why had she had to say he was wonderful and gifted? Did he *have* to be?

Something, a branch stirring in the breeze, or a bird

flying past, made me look up as I was passing the hill on Autumn Street where I'd first seen Hugh.

He had stood there on the top of the hill, holding on to a great scarlet kite in the sky. Later, I'd tied up my hair with a piece of the kite string. All the people on the street, Mrs. O'Connor and her children, the postman and old Mr. Thames, had been smiling. I had walked up the hill, and he'd come to me and started talking, and we'd had a conversation that had gone on for many months.

That morning, last year, even before I had waked up, Hugh was alone in his room, making the kite. Then he'd come to Autumn Street to fly it so that if it fell it wouldn't fall into the river. He hadn't known about me, Victoria Finch, or that I was going to write an assignment in English class he'd want to turn into a play, or that I was going to be his friend. He hadn't known Tom Kyle was going to move to New Oxford.

It had been chance. But what we had made of it, he and Tom and I, hadn't been chance.

I felt a great swoop of regret as though my heart, like the kite that morning, had fallen through space to the ground. I didn't want to feel that way any more. I hurried on toward home. But I looked back. Just once.